The Heart of the Aether

BOOK TWO OF THE AETHER SERIES

John Knight

ISBN 978-1-7641239-2-1

Printed in Australia
Second Edition -- Australian Version
First published in Australia by Silver Knight Press
www.silverknight.press

The Return of Aether

By John Knight

Table of Contents

Chapter One: A Whisper in the Dark

The days of celebration had faded, leaving behind the quiet hum of rebuilding. Pyrrha stood once more At the top of the castle walls, the morning sun casting a gentle light over the kingdom. The fields beyond the castle were green and fertile again, and the streets below were filled with the laughter of children playing and merchants calling out their wares. It was a world that had been born anew, from the ashes of war.

But even in the warmth of the sun, there was a chill that Pyrrha could not shake.

Aleron was beside her, as always, his presence a comfort, yet a shadow lingered between them—unsaid, unspoken. He, too, felt it. The quiet after the storm, the stillness before the next tempest.

"I should have known it wouldn't last," Pyrrha murmured, her fingers tracing the familiar hilt of her sword. Her father's words echoed in her mind: Peace is not a gift. It is a hard-earned battle, and even then, it is fragile.

Aleron squeezed her hand. "You have done more than anyone ever could. You have earned this peace, Pyrrha. We all have. Whatever comes next, we face it together."

She glanced at him, seeing the resolve in his eyes. She wanted to believe him, to let the weight of their past battles ease, but something tugged at her, a restlessness she could not deny. She could feel the tension building,

like the air before a storm. And that whisper, that faint voice from the shadows, refused to leave her thoughts.

"I hear something in the wind," she said softly, her gaze shifting to the horizon. "A warning. Something is coming, Aleron. I can feel it."

Before he could respond, the distant sound of a horn echoed through the long, mournful castle, its tone unnatural. It was a sound that had not been heard in years.

Pyrrha's heart skipped a beat. The kingdom was at peace. The land had been freed. What danger could be at their gates now?

Liora appeared at her side, her golden eyes narrowed, sensing the same unease. "Something stirs," she said, her voice grave. "It is not just the winds. There is a presence. Something old..."

Pyrrha's breath caught in her throat. Could it be the remnants of the dark forces she had defeated? Or was it something worse?

"Prepare the kingdom," Pyrrha ordered, her voice steady, though her heart was not. "Whatever this is, we face it head-on."

As she turned to walk toward the courtyard, the sky above seemed to darken for a moment, the winds picking up in a sudden gust. A shadow flitted across the sun, but when

Pyrrha looked up, there was nothing, only the vast, empty sky. But deep within her, she knew that something was coming. And this time, it would not be as easily defeated. The courtyard was already in motion by the time Pyrrha descended from the walls. Soldiers, knights, and advisors scrambled to their posts; their faces filled with a quiet sense of urgency. Aleron was by her side, though his usual calm demeanour seemed unsettled. He caught her arm gently, his voice low but firm.

"Pyrrha, this is not just a horn. I have heard it before," he said, eyes scanning the horizon as if searching for the source of the sound.

She met his gaze, and for the first time in a long while, Pyrrha saw a flicker of doubt in his eyes. It unsettled her.

"You've heard it before?" she repeated, her mind racing. "When? Where?"

He hesitated, his lips pressing into a thin line. "When I was young—before the kingdom fell into darkness. My father would tell us of an ancient order, long thought to have been erased. They would sound that same horn, calling something... something far older than we knew. I never understood it, not until now."

Pyrrha's grip tightened on the hilt of her sword. "What are you saying, Aleron?"

He took a deep breath, his voice steady. "I am saying that the horn is the signal of their return. The Order of the Silent Watchers." The name sent a shiver through

Pyrrha's spine. She had heard whispered rumours of this Order, a secretive faction of monks and sorcerers, believed to have been wiped out during the great wars long ago. No one knew what they truly sought, but there was rumoured to be vast, capable of changing the course of history.

But why now? Why after so many years of silence?

Liora appeared at Pyrrha's side, her golden eyes sharp and alert. "The Watchers are not just myth, Pyrrha," she said, her voice edged with concern. "Their purpose was always hidden in the shadows. But their influence... it could be far-reaching."

Aleron nodded, his jaw tightening. "We need to find out more, before they have a chance to strike."

Pyrrha turned her attention to the distance, where the sun was now fully set, casting an eerie glow over the landscape. There, on the far edge of the kingdom, the ancient forest lay—a vast expanse of trees that had long stood as a natural barrier between the kingdom and the unknown wilds beyond.

"Liora," Pyrrha said, her voice firm, "gather the council. Aleron, I need you to send word to the nearby kingdoms. We need allies—no one can stand against this Order alone."

Liora nodded without hesitation, her wings of radiant light flaring out for a moment before she vanished into the

gathering dusk. Aleron gave Pyrrha one last, lingering look

before hurrying of to execute her orders.

As Pyrrha moved through the courtyard, the quiet voices of her people surrounded her. They knew something was coming. They could feel it in the air, the tension thick and heavy. But none of them spoke of it, as if the mere mention would make it more real.

Pyrrha's mind raced, her thoughts a blur of strategy and uncertainty. Her kingdom had been saved, but she knew it could not remain untouched by the shadows forever. What was it that had awakened the Watchers now? And why had they waited so long?

She reached the edge of the castle grounds, where the path led into the dense woods. The ancient trees loomed ahead, their gnarled branches whispering in the wind, as if beckoning her forward.

A flicker of movement caught her eye—something dark and fleeting among the trees. Pyrrha's hand instinctively went to her sword, her body tensing, ready to strike. But when she looked again, there was nothing.

Nothing but the wind.

The feeling of being watched, of something just beyond her reach, lingered like a spectre. She could not shake it.

She knew she had no choice but to venture into the heart of the forest. The answers she sought lay beyond the kingdom's walls.

Her resolve hardened. No matter the cost, she would

uncover the truth. For her kingdom, for her people, and for the memory of her father.

With one final glance back at the castle, Pyrrha turned toward the trees, her footsteps steady, the weight of her sword a constant reminder of the battles yet to come.

Chapter Two: Into the Wild

The moon hung low in the sky, casting pale light over the dense forest. The wind rustled the leaves, but it was the silence that unnerved Pyrrha the most. It was not the absence of sound—there was always sound in the forest—but rather the unnatural stillness that had settled over everything. Even the usual cries of night creatures seemed absent.

Pyrrha's hand rested lightly on the hilt of her sword as she moved through the darkened undergrowth, each step carefully placed. Aleron had insisted on accompanying her, though she knew he, too, felt the weight of the unknown pressing on him. They were alone now, leaving the kingdom's borders behind, and with it, the fragile peace they had fought so hard to reclaim.

Beside her, Aleron was quiet, his face etched with a seriousness that Pyrrha rarely saw. He moved with ease through the shadows, his training as a prince in the art of diplomacy and strategy just as vital in this moment as any swordplay.

"The forest feels... different, doesn't it?" Aleron murmured, his voice barely above a whisper. "Like it's waiting for something."

"It's not just the forest," Pyrrha replied, her gaze shifting to the path ahead. "The Watchers have made their move. And I do not think we'll be alone much longer."

Aleron's eyes met hers, the unease in his expression mirrored by the tension in his posture. "You think they'll find us tonight?"

"Either tonight or very soon," Pyrrha said, her voice low, resolute. "The horn was no accident. They have been planning this. And they have waited long enough to strike."

They pressed on, the path winding deeper into the forest, where the trees seemed to grow taller, their trunks twisted and ancient. The air grew cooler, the scent of damp earth and moss thick around them. The only sound now was the crunch of leaves underfoot and the occasional whisper of wind between the branches.

Hours passed, and Pyrrha felt the weight of the journey settle over her. She could feel Aleron's presence at her side, though the quiet was heavy with unspoken words. Neither of them had said it aloud, but they both knew the danger that loomed ahead. If the Silent Watchers had returned, they wouldn't just be facing a threat to the kingdom—they would be up against something far older and more powerful than anything they had known.

Suddenly, Pyrrha stopped, her body tensing. Aleron, sensing the shift, halted beside her, his hand reaching instinctively for his sword.

"What is it?" he whispered.

Pyrrha's eyes darted around, scanning the shadows. For a moment, she felt as if the forest itself was holding its breath. Then, in the distance, a flicker of light appeared, barely visible between the thick trees. A soft glow, like fireflies—but it moved, and its rhythm was too deliberate to be natural.

"Something's coming," Pyrrha said, her voice steady despite the pulse of adrenaline rushing through her veins. "Stay close."

They crept forward, the glow growing brighter, and soon the source revealed itself. A figure stood at the edge of a clearing, cloaked in shadow, their silhouette outlined by the ethereal light they seemed to radiate. Pyrrha's breath caught in her throat.

It was not human.

The figure's features were obscured by the cloak, but Pyrrha could see the faint outline of something sharp, like a mask, just beneath the hood. Their presence exuded power, an unnatural energy that set her instincts on edge. The glow around them flickered, casting strange shadows that seemed to move of their own accord.

Aleron's grip tightened on his sword hilt. "What is that?"

"I don't know," Pyrrha said, her hand instinctively reaching for the hilt of her own sword. "But I've got a feeling it's connected to the Watchers."

Before either of them could make another move, the figure spoke, their voice a low, melodic hum that seemed to echo in the still air.

"You seek the truth, Princess," the figure said, their tone

carrying an ancient weight. "But truth has a price, and that price is never what you expect."

Pyrrha's eyes narrowed. "Who are you?"

The figure tilted their head slightly, the glow from beneath their hood shifting. "I am one of the Watchers, though not the one you seek. I am here to show you what lies beyond the veil, to guide you through the shadows of the past. But first, you must prove your worth."

A shiver ran down Pyrrha's spine. She could feel the weight of the words, the gravity of the choice that lay before her.

Aleron stepped forward, his voice firm. "We seek nothing but peace for the kingdom. If you are one of the Watchers, then you should know what we've been through. We've fought for this."

The figure's laugh was soft, almost sympathetic. "Peace? No, Prince. What you've fought for is nothing more than a brief respite. The storm that comes will shake the very foundation of your kingdom. The Watchers know of it, and we have waited… long enough."

Pyrrha's grip tightened on her sword. "If you know of the storm, then help us. Show us what is coming."

The figure's eyes gleamed beneath the hood, a spark of something ancient flickering in the depths. "The storm you face is not one of battle, Pyrrha. It is a storm of revelation. The truth will tear you apart."

Before she could respond, the figure's glow flared brightly, blinding Pyrrha for a moment. When her vision cleared, the figure was gone—vanished into the shadows as if they had never been there at all.

The silence of the forest returned, but it was no longer peaceful. A feeling of dread hung thick in the air, an unshakable weight that pressed down on Pyrrha's chest.

Aleron was the first to speak. "What was that? What do they want from us?"

"I don't know," Pyrrha said, her voice tight. "But we've just been given a warning... and a choice. The truth we're looking for is more dangerous than I thought. The Watchers are not our only problem."

She turned, her eyes scanning the now-empty clearing. "We need to find out more. We need to know what this storm truly is."

Chapter Three: The Edge of Truth

The forest seemed to close in around them as they made their way deeper into the heart of the wilderness. Every step Pyrrha took felt like it pulled her further away from the safety of the kingdom, farther from the peace they had fought so hard to regain. The night air was thick with the weight of unanswered questions.

Aleron was close beside her, his brow furrowed as he surveyed the path ahead. "Do you think it is possible that the Watchers are connected to the strange happenings in the kingdom? The rumours... the disappearances?"

Pyrrha nodded, but her mind raced. Her thoughts were a whirlwind of possibilities, none of them offering much comfort. The Watchers had always been a myth; a whispered tale told around campfires to children too young to understand the true darkness of the world. But now, they were no longer just stories. They were real, and their intentions were anything but clear.

"They are connected," Pyrrha said, her voice firm. "But what their connection is... I don't know yet. All I do know is that they are not just guardians of the past—they are tied to something much darker, something older than even my father's reign."

Aleron stopped walking for a moment, looking at her with concern. "Pyrrha, whatever this is, we will face it together. But you don't have to carry this burden alone."

Pyrrha turned to face him, her heart heavy with the weight of his words. She could feel his concern, his loyalty, but part of her—the warrior, the daughter of the fallen king—couldn't help but feel the pull of the journey. She had started this quest alone, and perhaps it was better to finish it that way.

"I know, Aleron," she said, her voice soft but resolute. "But some burdens are meant to be carried alone. There are truths I must uncover, things that my father left behind. And some of them... may be too dangerous for anyone but me."

Aleron didn't argue, but there was an undeniable sadness in his eyes. He had seen the toll her past had taken on her, and he feared the weight of the path she was now walking.

They continued onward in silence, the dense trees offering little light under the clouded sky. The only sounds were the crunch of their footsteps and the occasional call of a distant owl.

It wasn't long before they arrived at the edge of a clearing. In the centre stood a crumbling stone structure, half-consumed by the roots of ancient trees. The remnants of a once-proud temple, long abandoned by those who had built it.

"This is it," Pyrrha murmured. "The Temple of Veils."

Aleron looked at the structure with a mix of awe and apprehension. "You think the Watchers are here?"

"I don't think it, I know it," she replied. "This place was

sacred to them. And it's no coincidence that we've found it now."

They stepped into the clearing, their boots soft against the overgrown grass. The temple's walls were covered in ivy, its stones etched with symbols Pyrrha had seen in old texts—symbols of forgotten magic, binding rituals, and the deep secrets of the world.

As they entered the temple's shadow, a sudden gust of wind swept through the clearing, and Pyrrha froze. A distant voice, as faint as a whisper on the breeze, reached her ears. It was no ordinary voice. It was the same voice she had heard in the forest, the voice of the Watcher.

"The truth lies within," the voice called, echoing from all directions. "But so does your doom."

Pyrrha's heart skipped a beat, and she instinctively reached for her sword, her senses heightened. The temple seemed to pulse with an energy she could not understand—an ancient magic that made her skin prickle with anticipation.

Aleron stepped closer, his hand resting on his own blade. "Are we meant to go in?"

"Only one way to find out," Pyrrha replied, her voice steady. She took a deep breath and stepped forward, feeling the weight of the temple's history pressing down on her shoulders. "We need to know what the Watchers want. And we need to find the answers."

The moment they crossed the threshold, the atmosphere

inside the temple shifted. The air grew thick, almost suffocating. The walls, once faded with age, seemed to come alive with a glow that pulsed in rhythm with Pyrrha's heartbeat. The symbols on the stone walls shifted before her eyes, rearranging themselves like a puzzle she was meant to solve.

In the centre of the temple lay a raised platform, where a stone altar stood, covered in moss and dust. But it was not the altar that drew Pyrrha's attention—it was the faint shimmer of something just beyond it, barely visible to the naked eye.

A glow, soft yet bright, emanated from the shadows, calling to her like a siren's song. She stepped forward, her heart pounding in her chest, the pull of the light stronger with each passing moment. But as she neared, the air seemed to grow colder, and the symbols on the walls twisted violently.

Then, a voice—not the Watcher's, but something far darker—rang out, sharp and clear.

"You dare disturb the past, child?"

Pyrrha's blood ran cold.

She spun around, her sword drawn, but there was no one there. The temple was silent again, the eerie glow fading.

Aleron's voice was urgent. "Pyrrha, we need to leave. Something is wrong."

But Pyrrha could not tear her gaze away from the spot where

the voice had come from. She felt the presence— something ancient, something powerful. Something that had been waiting.

"We can't leave," she said, her voice barely a whisper. "We've come too far."

As she stepped closer to the altar, the air crackled with energy. The stone beneath her feet seemed to vibrate, and the symbols on the walls shimmered once more, now more intense, more alive than ever.

The truth was within this temple. But so, too, was something far more dangerous than Pyrrha had ever anticipated.

Chapter Four: The Power of Unity

The air in the temple seemed to close in around them, the weight of its ancient energy pressing against Pyrrha's chest. Her heart pounded; her senses heightened as though the very stones beneath her feet were alive with the past's whispers. The voice that had spoken was not one she could ignore. It had carried a weight, a warning, and the presence that accompanied it was darker than anything she had encountered before.

Aleron stepped closer, his eyes narrowing with concern. "Pyrrha, we need to be careful. This place is more dangerous than we thought. Whatever is here… it is not just the Watchers. There is something else."

Pyrrha did not answer right away. Her gaze remained fixed on the altar, the faint shimmer growing in intensity with each passing second. She could feel it now—the pull. It was not just the temple's ancient magic she felt. It was a connection, a thread woven between her and Aleron, stronger than it had ever been before. It was as if their destinies were intertwined in a way that went beyond coincidence.

She glanced at him, and their eyes met. There was no mistaking it now. In the silence between them, they both knew. They were not just allies in battle, but two souls bound together by fate. The realization settled over her like a cloak—heavy yet comforting.

"What if it's us?" she asked softly, her voice trembling just a little, though she didn't quite understand why. "What if… we're meant to face this together? Not just as warriors, but as something more?"

Aleron seemed to pause for a long moment, his gaze fixed on her with a mixture of awe and uncertainty. "You mean… as more than just comrades?"

Pyrrha nodded slowly, her breath shallow. "Yes. I think… our connection goes deeper than I realised. The power between us—it feels stronger now, like it is drawing us together. It is as if our bond is the key to understanding what's happening here."

Aleron stepped forward, closer to her, the distance between them closing, both physically and emotionally. His eyes softened, the tension in them replaced by something else—something tender yet filled with determination. "I feel it, too. But Pyrrha… is this the right time? Are we ready for this?"

Pyrrha hesitated, but only for a heartbeat. She had carried the weight of her father's legacy alone for so long, shouldering every decision, every burden. But now, with Aleron beside her, she realised that carrying it alone was not the answer. Together, they would face whatever lay ahead.

"I've been afraid of relying on anyone," she admitted, her voice barely a whisper. "Afraid that if I let someone in… it would make me weak. But I see now. We are stronger together. We always have been."

The glow of the temple flickered again, as if in response to her words. The ancient energy in the air hummed, alive with the magic that was now awakening between them. She could feel it, like an electric current flowing through her veins, amplifying her strength, her focus. And she could feel it in Aleron, too—his pulse quickened, his breath shallow.

He reached out, taking her hand gently in his. "Then we do this together. We face whatever is coming—not as two individuals, but as a pair. United."

For a moment, nothing else existed but the sound of their breathing and the intensity of the connection they shared. Pyrrha could feel the power between them, growing stronger with each passing second. This bond was not just emotional—it was magical, a force that resonated deep within their souls. And as they stood there, hand in hand, she knew that this was only the beginning of what they could accomplish together.

A sudden tremor ran through the temple, shaking the stone beneath their feet. The symbols on the walls glowed brighter, and the air crackled with energy. It was as if the temple itself had recognized the bond between them, and in that moment, Pyrrha knew—there was no turning back.

"We can't turn back now," she said, her voice filled with determination. "We are in this together. Whatever happens next, we face it together."

Aleron nodded, his grip on her hand tightening. "Together."

The air around them seemed to shift, the oppressive energy of the temple pulsing like a heartbeat. The altar ahead shimmered with an ethereal glow, and the ground beneath them began to tremble once more.

Pyrrha drew her sword, the flames along its blade flickering as if in response to the rising power in the air. Aleron's hand rested on his own sword, his stance ready for whatever came next.

They stood together, side by side, as the power of the temple—and the strength of their newfound bond—swelled around them.

Something ancient and powerful was awakening, and it was drawing them into its grasp. But they would not face it alone. Together, they would fight. Together, they would uncover the truth.

And together, they would stand against whatever darkness rose to challenge them.

Chapter Five: A Bond Forged in Flame

The dark figure's laugh echoed in the chamber, sending a shiver down Pyrrha's spine. But even as the walls seemed to close in, she stood firm. Her sword flickered with fire, the flames glowing hotter with every beat of her heart.

Aleron stood beside her, his weapon drawn and eyes locked on the figure in front of them. But there was something more now—something she could feel, like a soft pulse in her chest. It was as if Aleron's heartbeat in time with hers, as if their thoughts were starting to align.

"What are you waiting for?" the figure sneered. "Come, fight me if you dare. But I warn you, you will fail."

Pyrrha gritted her teeth. "Not today."

In that moment, something shifted—something Pyrrha could not explain. She felt a wave of warmth spread through her, not from the flames of her sword, but from somewhere deeper. It was as though a part of her soul was opening, a connection forming between her and Aleron.

She glanced at him, and to her surprise, he met her gaze with a knowing look. His eyes were not just filled with determination—they were filled with understanding. As if he knew exactly what she was thinking.

She didn't need to speak the words, and neither did he.

Together.

It wasn't just a vow—it was a certainty. In that instant, Pyrrha felt the bond between them, an invisible thread that linked their minds and hearts. They did not need to communicate with words, or even gestures. Their thoughts, their intentions, moved as one. It was as if the very essence of their beings were in harmony, a perfect synchronization of will.

In her mind, she felt Aleron's thoughts as clearly as her own. We fight together. Every move, every breath, we are one.

She nodded, feeling his resolve strengthen her own. Their connection was so deep now, so entwined, that she could sense the shifting of his thoughts, the planning of their next steps—before he even moved.

The figure before them sneered once more. "You think this connection will save you? You are both too weak. You cannot fight me alone, let alone together."

But Pyrrha and Aleron already knew the truth. They did not need to fight alone. Their minds—combined—were sharper than any blade, their plans more calculated than any strategy they could devise separately.

We move as one, Pyrrha thought.

Aleron's presence in her mind was a steady warmth, his determination a constant heartbeat beside hers. Without a word, they both shifted their stance, moving fluidly as if they had rehearsed it a thousand times. The figure's sneer faltered for a split second, but it was enough.

With a unified strike, Pyrrha lunged forward, the fire of her sword trailing behind her like a comet's tail. Aleron followed in perfect rhythm, his sword an extension of her own, their combined force overwhelming the dark magic that had threatened to consume them.

The dark figure raised his hand in a final, desperate attempt to unleash his power, but Pyrrha felt Aleron's thoughts before the attack even began. Not yet. We wait.

They danced around the figure, their movements becoming one continuous flow. Every time the figure struck, they were already in motion, anticipating his every move. It was as if they had become two halves of a single whole. Their movements were fluid, graceful—precise.

And when the figure finally staggered, disoriented and weary from the barrage of attacks, Pyrrha felt the pulse in her chest—the signal.

Now.

With a cry that echoed through the chamber, they struck simultaneously. Pyrrha's sword and Aleron's blade met the dark figure's chest at the same time. The force of their combined strength sent a shockwave through the temple, knocking the figure to his knees.

He gasped for breath, his form flickering like a dying flame. "You think you've won?" he rasped, his voice barely a whisper now. "You cannot erase the past."

But Pyrrha was resolute. "The past will not control me. We are the future."

With one final strike, the dark figure was silenced. His form dissolved into nothingness, and the oppressive energy in the temple vanished, leaving only the lingering echo of his final words.

For a long moment, there was nothing but silence—thick, heavy silence.

And then, slowly, Pyrrha turned to Aleron. The bond between them was still strong, their minds still linked, but now, it felt... different. More solid, more certain.

She felt the warmth of his presence like a steady flame within her chest. And as their eyes met, she knew.

They were no longer just two warriors fighting side by side. They were two halves of a whole, their connection stronger than any force they could face.

"We did it," Pyrrha whispered, her voice filled with awe.

Aleron nodded, his expression softening as he took a step closer. "We did it together."

And in that moment, they knew there was nothing they could not face as long as they remained one.

Chapter Six: The Quiet Before the Storm

The weeks that followed the battle in the temple were peaceful—unsettlingly so. Pyrrha could not shake the feeling that something was just out of place. The air was still, as if the world itself were holding its breath, waiting for something terrible to emerge from the shadows. Yet the kingdom thrived. People celebrated, the land flourished, and Aleron and Pyrrha grew closer, their bond deepening with every passing day.

But the tranquillity felt fragile, a thin veil over something darker lurking beneath.

One evening, as they sat by the fire in their quarters, the warmth of their bond flowing between them, Pyrrha's brow furrowed. She could not shake the sense of unease that had been gnawing at her for days.

Aleron, sensing her change in demeanour, turned to her, his gaze gentle but piercing. "What is it?"

"I can't explain it," she said, voice low, "but something feels wrong. The figure we faced in the temple... he is gone, but I can't help but feel he's still out there."

Aleron's eyes darkened as he met her gaze. "You feel it too?"

"Yes. It is like a shadow—always just out of reach. But I know he has not been destroyed."

Aleron nodded, placing his hand over hers. The warmth of

his touch calmed her, but only for a moment. He understood her completely; their minds still entwined in the way they had come to rely on.

"We need to stay vigilant," he said, the words heavy with a sense of finality. "If he is still out there, we will face him again. But this time, we will not be caught off guard."

Pyrrha's heart ached with the knowledge that their victory had been short-lived. The darkness they had fought so hard to defeat would not remain gone forever. But she wasn't afraid—not anymore. Together, they were stronger. And as their connection grew, she knew they could face anything, even the return of their most dangerous foe.

But it was then—a whisper in the back of her mind—that she felt it.

A cold, familiar presence.

It was faint, just a flutter of dark energy, like a ripple on the surface of an otherwise still pond. But it was enough.

"He's coming," Pyrrha whispered, her voice trembling with the knowledge that the battle was far from over.

Aleron stood in one fluid motion, his sword appearing in his hand as though summoned by his thoughts. He stepped toward her, his eyes narrowed, a mixture of determination and something else... fear, perhaps, or the weight of responsibility that had settled on their shoulders since they'd realised the truth of their connection.

"We won't let him destroy us," Aleron said, his voice calm,

yet filled with an intensity that only Pyrrha could fully understand.

She nodded, her gaze flickering to the window, where the moonlight bathed the land in silver. Somewhere, out there in the night, their enemy waited. Watching. Biding his time.

Their bond pulsed between them—familiar, warm, and reassuring—but beneath it, there was something else. A sense of dread. Of an approaching storm they were not yet prepared to weather.

But they would face it together.

Just as they always had.

Chapter Seven: The Heart's True Power

The moon hung high above them, a brilliant silver orb in the clear night sky, casting soft shadows across the land. It had been days since the last battle. The enemy, though ever-present in their minds, had receded, for now at least. For the first time in a long while, Pyrrha and Aleron were granted a moment of respite—a chance to rest, to breathe, to be themselves away from the constant weight of war.

They sat by the fire, the warmth of the flames mingling with the cool breeze that danced through the trees. Pyrrha leaned against Aleron, her head resting on his shoulder as he absently ran his fingers through her hair. It was a simple act, but one that felt like a lifeline in the midst of the chaos. The world, for this brief moment, felt still. The silence between them was comfortable, heavy with unspoken words.

"I never thought I'd find peace like this again," Pyrrha whispered, her voice barely audible over the crackling of the fire.

Aleron's voice was just as soft as he answered, "It feels like a dream, doesn't it?"

Pyrrha nodded. "I almost don't know how to feel about it. After everything, after all the loss, and the battles... this peace feels too fragile."

Aleron shifted slightly, turning to face her, his hand cupping her cheek gently. "It's not fragile," he said, his voice firm but tender. "It's earned."

The way he said it—so certain, so sure—stirred something deep inside Pyrrha. It was more than just the words; it was the weight of everything they had been through, together. The sacrifices, the losses, the victories. And now, this calm. This fleeting moment where they could simply be.

Their eyes met, and for a heartbeat, the world outside seemed to disappear. All that existed was the connection between them. It was stronger now than ever before, their bond solidified through shared battles, shared grief, and shared triumphs. They could feel each other—hear each other's thoughts without speaking.

Aleron's gaze softened as his thumb brushed across her lower lip. "Pyrrha, I... I have never felt more alive than when I'm with you. This journey we have taken together— it's been everything I never knew I needed."

The words felt like a confession, a truth that had been building for a long time but had never fully been expressed. Pyrrha felt her heartbeat faster at the sincerity in his voice. She had known, of course—known the depth of her feelings for him—but hearing him speak the words aloud made everything feel real. More than real. It made her feel whole.

"I feel the same way," she whispered back, her voice trembling slightly. "But Aleron, we have so much more to face. So many battles still ahead of us."

Aleron smiled, but there was a quiet sadness in his eyes. "We do. But we will face them together, as we always have. And if that means I must fight beside you, in every sense of the word, then I will do so. There is no place I'd rather be."

A warmth spread through Pyrrha's chest at his words. The power they shared, the strength they had built together, was undeniable. She could feel it now—an energy that surged between them, stronger than anything they had experienced before. It was not just the magic, or the battles they had won. It was the depth of their connection. The trust, the understanding. The love.

And in that moment, she knew. Now is the time.

She leaned in, closing the distance between them, her lips brushing against his with a softness that sent a shiver through both of them. It was not rushed, but inevitable. The kiss deepened, slow and steady, as if their very souls were intertwined. The fire between them burned hotter than the flames that crackled at their feet.

When they finally pulled apart, breathless, Pyrrha's eyes sparkled with something new—something fierce. "Aleron... I want this. With you."

He did not speak at first, only nodded, his gaze intense and unwavering. He could feel it too—the undeniable pull, the need to be closer, to share more than just their thoughts.

There, in the quiet of the night, amidst the stillness of their sanctuary, they came together—not just as allies, but as two souls bound by more than fate.

As their bodies joined in the most intimate way, a surge of power coursed through them, like an invisible tide that swept through every fibre of their being. It was as if the magic they shared grew exponentially, a force that transcended mere battle. The bond between them was unbreakable now, their unity more than just a connection of thoughts. It was a bond forged in love, trust, and power—an unshakable foundation that would see them through whatever came next.

When the storm returned, and it would return, they would face it not as two individuals, but as one—a force unlike any the world had ever seen.

Chapter Eight: Shadows Stir

The morning after their union was unlike any Pyrrha had ever known. The air felt lighter, the world brighter, as though the very earth itself was rejoicing in their bond. The power they had shared, the connection that had deepened between them, lingered like a quiet hum, strengthening them in ways they had not yet fully understood.

They woke to the sound of birds singing and the scent of the forest all around them, but beneath the calm serenity of the day, Pyrrha could not shake the sense that something was still wrong. As if the calm before a storm was drawing near, and they were standing at its edge without knowing.

Aleron stirred beside her, his arm draped over her, the warmth of his presence grounding her. When his eyes fluttered open, the quiet morning light caught in his hair, his gaze soft but filled with a quiet intensity that made Pyrrha's heart flutter, even now.

"Good morning," he whispered, his voice still husky from sleep.

She smiled, running her fingers through his hair. "It feels like the world is different, doesn't it? After last night."

"It does," he agreed, his voice tinged with wonder. "I feel... more. More connected to you, to everything. It's like the bond between us is stronger than I ever could have imagined."

Pyrrha nodded, her heart swelling. It was more than just the magic, more than just the power of their connection. It was the depth of their shared experience, their trust, and their love.

But as they lay there, together in the quiet of the morning, the air around them seemed to shift. The stillness, once comforting, began to feel oppressive. The weight of the world settled back upon Pyrrha's shoulders, the memories of their enemies and the battles yet to come creeping into her thoughts.

"I have to ask you something," Aleron said, his tone serious now, the playfulness from earlier gone. "Do you feel it too?"

Pyrrha hesitated, her eyes meeting his. "Feel what?"

"The... presence. Something is of. I can't explain it, but it's like the air itself is holding its breath, waiting for something to happen."

Her pulse quickened. She had felt it too—an unease that had nothing to do with their immediate surroundings. It was a deeper, more unsettling feeling. The echo of something that had never truly been vanquished, something that still lingered in the shadows.

"I do," Pyrrha admitted, sitting up slowly, her senses alert. "It's as if the danger we faced hasn't entirely passed. It feels like something is waiting to return."

Aleron sat up beside her, his hand finding hers. "We need to be ready."

Pyrrha nodded, her thoughts already racing. "We'll be ready. Together."

They stood in silence for a moment, their eyes meeting in shared resolve. There was no denying it now. They had faced many dangers, but this new threat, this shadow that loomed just beyond their reach, was something else entirely. It was not just an enemy they could see or fight— it was something deeper, more insidious. A force that might seek to tear them apart, not through force of arms, but through deception, through manipulation.

Pyrrha could feel the weight of what was to come pressing down on her. But this time, she would not face it alone.

Aleron's hand tightened around hers. "Whatever it is, we'll face it together. We always have."

Pyrrha smiled softly, the strength of their bond surging through her. "Together. Always."

The rest of the day passed in a blur of preparations. Pyrrha and Aleron worked in unspoken unity, preparing their camp, their weapons, and their minds for what lay ahead. But even as they went through the motions, something was shifting inside them. The magic they shared, the power they had gained from their bond, was growing stronger. But it was not just the magic. It was the connection—the trust—that held them steady. It was their

hearts, now beating in sync, and it would be this bond that

would see them through whatever darkness awaited them.

That evening, as they sat around the fire, a feeling of foreboding settled over them. The night was quiet, too quiet, as if the world itself was holding its breath.

And then, just as they were about to retire for the night, a strange sound pierced the air.

A whisper, faint but unmistakable, floated on the wind.

It was a voice. Not one they recognized. But it was close. Too close.

The voice was soft, like a murmur in the back of the mind, curling around them like smoke.

"The past has a way of coming back… and you, Pyrrha, have only just begun to understand the power of your destiny."

The air grew cold, the flames of the fire flickering and dancing wildly.

Pyrrha's heart stopped in her chest. She looked at Aleron, their shared connection sparking as their minds both registered the same realization.

It had returned.

Chapter Nine: The Echoes of Fate

The voice lingered in the air, its words heavy with an ominous weight. It was as if the very fabric of the world itself had shifted, and Pyrrha felt it deep within her soul. The flame of the campfire flickered once more before burning brightly, casting erratic shadows across the clearing. It was a reminder that the calm they had shared had been fleeting—a false tranquillity.

Aleron rose to his feet, his eyes scanning the night. "Did you hear that too?" His voice was low, tight with concern, but there was a fire in his eyes. He had never been one to shy away from danger, but this was different. This felt personal. This felt like something from the depths of their shared past.

Pyrrha nodded slowly, her heart pounding in her chest. "I heard it. But who—what—was that?"

She stood, her senses sharpening, and instinctively reached for her sword. The familiar weight of the blade was a comfort, but even as her fingers closed around the hilt, she felt something stir within her—an unsettling pull that resonated deep within her.

Aleron turned his gaze to her, his hand reaching for hers. The moment their fingers intertwined, a surge of magic pulsed between them, a current of shared energy that seemed to hum in the air. It was as if their connection had grown even more potent, and with it, the sense that something was watching them—waiting.

"Pyrrha," Aleron's voice was firm, but there was a quiet urgency in it. "Whatever this is, it's not just about us anymore. It is something much larger, something ancient. We need to understand it before it consumes us."

She met his gaze, the unspoken understanding passing between them. They had faced threats before, but this was different. This time, it was not just a battle of strength or magic. This was a challenge that went to the very core of their destiny, and neither of them could walk away from it.

"We'll face it together," Pyrrha said, her voice resolute, steady. "We've always faced everything together."

Aleron nodded, his expression hardening with resolve. "And we always will."

But as they shared the moment of unbreakable connection, the very ground beneath them seemed to tremble. A low, guttural rumble echoed through the forest, and the shadows of the trees stretched longer, darker, as if they were reaching toward them. The air thickened, charged with an unnatural energy.

Then, from the darkness beyond their campfire's glow, a figure emerged.

It was tall, cloaked in black robes that seemed to shimmer with a strange, otherworldly light. Its face was hidden beneath a hood, but the air around it crackled with

malevolent power. Pyrrha felt a chill run through her, as

though the very essence of death had come to greet them.

"Pyrrha Infernal," the figure spoke, its voice a low rasp, echoing with a strange, familiar resonance. "You think you've won. You think your journey has ended. But your destiny is far from over. It has only just begun."

Aleron stepped in front of Pyrrha, his hand instinctively reaching for the hilt of his sword, but the figure raised a hand, and the air around them seemed to freeze. Pyrrha could feel the oppressive weight of magic suffocating them, the power of the figure's presence pressing in from all sides.

"Who are you?" Pyrrha demanded, her voice steady despite the fear creeping into her bones. She could feel Aleron's grip tightening around her hand, their connection flaring with a protective instinct. Together, they were stronger than ever.

The figure chuckled, a sound that sent shivers down Pyrrha's spine. "I am no one, and I am everyone. I have waited long enough. And now, Pyrrha, you will understand. You will know the truth about your bloodline, the truth about your father."

The name "father" hit Pyrrha like a punch to the gut. Her mind raced, recalling the lessons he had taught her, the love and sacrifices he had made. Her father had been her guiding light, the reason for everything she fought for. "Your father," the figure continued, its voice now dripping with malicious pleasure, "was a fool. He thought he could protect you from the truth, but the truth is a force that cannot be hidden forever. It will find you, Pyrrha. And when it does, it will break you."

Aleron moved closer to her, his presence grounding her, but the figure's power weighed them both down, as if it had its grip around their very souls.

"What do you want from us?" Pyrrha demanded, her sword now drawn, flames dancing along its edge. She could feel the heat of the blade in her hand, a comforting reminder that she had the strength to fight. But something told her that this battle would not be won with steel alone.

The figure tilted its head slightly, the hood casting its face in deeper shadows. "I want nothing from you. You, however, will be the one to decide. Will you continue to run from the truth? Or will you face it, and in doing so, embrace your true destiny?"

The tension in the air was palpable, and Pyrrha could feel the weight of the decision that lay before her. This figure—this presence—knew too much. It had been watching them, waiting for the right moment. The truth about her father, the truth about her bloodline—what was it that had been hidden from her all this time?

The figure's presence lingered for a moment longer before it slowly began to dissipate, the shadows it cast stretching and bending unnaturally before it vanished entirely. The air grew still, the oppressive weight, lifting as quickly as it had come.

Pyrrha stood frozen, her heart racing, her mind spinning

with the implications of what had just happened.

Aleron's voice broke the silence, his tone low and filled with concern. "Pyrrha, what was that? Who was that?"

Pyrrha shook her head, her mind reeling. "I don't know... but I have a feeling it's only the beginning."

Her grip tightened around her sword. There was more to her father's legacy than she had ever been told. And whatever it was, it was going to come for her. And this time, she had no choice but to face it head-on.

Chapter Ten: The Weight of Shadows

The world outside seemed impossibly still. The quiet after the storm, a moment that felt suspended between the past and what was to come. Pyrrha stood before the great stone fireplace in the castle's chamber, the crackling fire casting warm light against the cold walls. Yet, despite the warmth, a chill lingered in her heart—a gnawing sense that no matter how many victories she achieved, the darkness had not been vanquished.

She had faced the threat of dark magic before, and it had nearly consumed her. But this... this felt different. Aleron's words echoed in her mind, his voice thick with concern, urging her to trust in their bond. But trusting him was no longer the only challenge. It was trusting herself, accepting the depths of the power they shared and what it would mean for their future.

Her hand tightened around the sword resting against the stone hearth, its fiery edge dull in the low light. She had fought for so long, driven by vengeance, by a need to avenge her father and protect those she loved. But now... now, her motives were more complicated. She had found herself standing at a precipice, no longer certain where the path of justice ended and where her desires began.

A sound behind her made her stiffen—Aleron's presence was unmistakable. She did not need to turn to know he was there, his familiar warmth enveloping the room like a shield. He had been there for her through every storm, but now, it seemed as though they were both adrift in a sea of unknowns, neither of them fully in control.

"You've been quiet," Aleron said, his voice low, soft. "Too quiet."

She finally turned to him, her eyes meeting his. The look he gave her was one of concern, yet there was something deeper in the way he gazed at her—an understanding that went beyond words. It was the same understanding they had shared during their time together, that connection that had grown between them. But this time, she felt the weight of it differently. He was not just the prince now; he was a part of her, and that bond was something she couldn't ignore.

"I'm not sure I can do this, Aleron," Pyrrha admitted, her voice trembling slightly. "This... this responsibility. I am afraid of what's coming. Of what it will ask of me."

Aleron stepped closer, his hand reaching out to gently cup her cheek. The touch was grounding, warm, as though he were pulling her back from a place she hadn't even realised she had slipped into—a place of doubt and fear.

"You don't have to do it alone, Pyrrha," he whispered, his forehead resting against hers. "We are together in this. We have always been. And we will always be. Whatever comes next, we face it together."

For a moment, the world outside seemed to fade away. The fire crackled softly, the night air still, the distant whispers of the kingdom's unrest muted. In that moment,

Pyrrha allowed herself to feel the weight of the connection they had forged—no longer just a partnership of necessity, but a bond of deep, undeniable understanding. Their minds and hearts were aligned in a way that transcended mere words, an intimacy that no external force could break.

She closed her eyes, taking a steadying breath, leaning into his warmth. His presence was a lifeline, a reminder that even in the darkest moments, they were stronger together.

"I don't know if I can protect you from what's coming, Aleron," Pyrrha whispered, the fear in her voice palpable. "I don't know what this all means for us."

Aleron's fingers brushed through her hair gently, his thumb brushing her cheek in a silent promise. "You don't have to protect me, Pyrrha. We protect each other. We are one now—our hearts, our thoughts, everything. Whatever darkness comes, it will never stand against us. Not now. Not ever."

The depth of his words, the raw sincerity in his gaze, broke through the last of her walls. She leaned into him, their foreheads touching now, breaths mingling as they stood in perfect silence. It was not the comfort of a lover's embrace, but the steady strength of two souls bound together by fate, by choice, by the very fire that burned within them both.

And in that quiet moment, she realised something that she had known all along but had not allowed herself too fully accept until now: their connection was more than just shared power. It was the foundation of something greater—something unbreakable. They were not just partners in battle. They were partners in life. In every sense.

The firelight flickered around them, casting dancing shadows against the walls, but Pyrrha felt the weight of the shadows lift. They were no longer just two warriors facing an uncertain future. They were a force. Together, they were unstoppable.

"You're right," she whispered, her voice strong now, her resolve returning. "We will face it together."

Aleron's lips brushed against her forehead, a soft, reverent gesture, and she felt her heart steady, the tumult within her fading as they stood in perfect union, ready to face whatever came next.

As they pulled away, the firelight glinted of the edge of her sword once more, its glow now a reflection of the light within her. Whatever darkness sought to rise again; she would meet it head-on—with Aleron by her side.

Chapter Eleven: Fractured Threads

The night had fallen heavy, the winds whispering strange, restless secrets through the trees. Pyrrha and Aleron sat by the campfire, its flickering light casting long shadows on their faces, their once solid bond of unity feeling like a thin thread.

The air between them was thick with an unsettling silence. They had just come from a battle—their victory hard-won but costly. A feeling lingered in Pyrrha's chest, something gnawing at her, a sense of something not quite right.

"I don't understand," Aleron's voice broke the silence, the pain in his words cutting through the stillness. "I thought we were ready. I thought we could handle it all together."

Pyrrha's brow furrowed as she turned to him, her heart heavy with concern. "What do you mean?"

Aleron's hand trembled as he reached for hers. His eyes were clouded with confusion, uncertainty. "The connection—between us. It is... fading. I can't hear your thoughts like I used to. It's like there's a wall between us, one I can't break through."

A shiver ran down Pyrrha's spine, and she quickly squeezed his hand, but the knot in her chest tightened. "I feel it too. But we have faced worse before. This is just another test. We can fight through it."

Her words were stronger than she felt. Deep inside, a cold

fear gripped her heart. The bond they had cultivated, that had been their strength, was faltering, and she did not know why. She had not felt this kind of isolation since the early days of their journey.

Suddenly, a voice echoed through the air, an insidious whisper that seemed to come from every direction, curling into their minds like a serpent.

"How long can you hold onto something so fragile, Pyrrha? Can love truly to protect you from the inevitable? Do you not see that you are weak without me? You are nothing but pawns, chasing a shadow of a future that will never be yours."

The voice was alien, cold, and malicious. It did not come from Aleron, and yet it felt like it was within him, his mind an open door to the voice's poison.

Pyrrha stood, heart racing, her sword already in hand, her gaze darting around the camp. "Who's there? Show yourself!"

Aleron stood too, but his expression was one of distant confusion, his brow furrowed as if battling something inside himself. "Pyrrha... I don't... I don't know why, but I cannot see you clearly. You're fading from my mind."

Her pulse thundered in her ears, panic threatening to rise. The fire crackled, casting flickering shadows that seemed to distort around them. The air itself seemed to warp, bending and shifting in strange ways, warping reality.

"You cannot win this fight, Pyrrha," the voice continued,

colder now, almost gloating. "I've been in your head for longer than you realise. The love between you and Aleron is your greatest weakness. Let it go. You will be stronger alone. You know it's true. You've always been alone."

The cold words seeped into her, filling her with doubt. Was this true? Could she be stronger without Aleron? Hadn't she fought alone for so long before he had come into her life? Aleron's power had only grown through their connection—but could they really continue to rely on each other?

"Aleron..." Pyrrha whispered, her voice trembling. The connection—the bond—felt so far away now, like a distant memory. She could barely sense him now, his presence a faint echo at the back of her mind.

"I... I don't know what is happening," Aleron said, his voice cracking, his eyes filled with desperation. "I can't feel you. I do not want to lose you, Pyrrha. Please."

In that moment, a deep ache pulsed in her heart. No. I cannot lose him. Not now, not ever.

But the voice continued, relentless in its manipulation. "You don't belong together. You are both too weak to survive this. The darkness will claim you in the end."

The fire in front of them flickered violently, casting eerie shadows as the voice's hold on them grew stronger, pulling them farther apart. Pyrrha's head spun with

confusion and uncertainty, her once unshakable resolve now questioned.

"Aleron, we need to fight this. Together," Pyrrha's voice trembled but remained firm. "Don't listen to it. Whatever this is, it's not real."

Aleron's eyes met hers, a flicker of recognition sparking in them. "I... I can feel you, Pyrrha. But it's so weak. It's like something is trying to tear us apart."

Pyrrha closed her eyes, reaching out, her breath shaky. She could feel his presence, faint but there. She clung to it, to the warmth of it, the strength of it. This connection is real. It's stronger than any enemy.

"Listen to me," she whispered, her voice urgent and raw. "We are stronger together. We chose this bond. Nothing can take that from us."

In that moment, their eyes met, and something flickered between them—a spark of understanding, of mutual recognition. They were one, and nothing could take that away.

The enemy's voice faltered, a brief crack in its icy grip. Pyrrha reached for Aleron's hand, their fingers intertwining, their thoughts synchronizing, their connection pushing back against the darkness.

The darkness shrieked, like a thousand voices crying out in agony, but it did not break. Not yet.

Pyrrha took a step closer to Aleron, her heart steadying as their minds connected, stronger than before, their bond flaring back to life. "We will fight this," she said, her voice resolute. "And we will win."

But the presence in the shadows had only just begun to make its move. This was not the end. It was only the beginning.

Chapter Twelve: A Shifting Tide

The days that followed the battle were heavy with uncertainty. Though the immediate threat had subsided, the presence that haunted their minds lingered like a dark cloud. The connection Pyrrha and Aleron had fought so hard to reclaim remained fragile, a flickering flame in the wind.

The journey ahead had become even more perilous. Pyrrha could feel the strain in her chest every time their minds drifted apart, and though they fought to stay united, the enemy that plagued them seemed to know their every move, every vulnerability. It was as if the darkness could sense the fractures in their bond, growing stronger with each passing hour.

Still, they pressed forward.

"Pyrrha," Aleron's voice was soft as they trudged through the thick, mist-laden forest. His hand brushed hers, a brief touch that spoke volumes. "We can't let this divide us."

Pyrrha looked over at him, her expression one of determination but weary concern. "I know. But something about this feels different. It's more than just an enemy. It's as if it's trying to tear us apart—physically, mentally, everything."

Aleron nodded, his brow furrowing. "Whatever it is, it's smart. It's playing on our fears, our doubts." He paused for a moment before adding, "I can feel it, Pyrrha. I feel it inside me. It's not just in our minds anymore. It's like it's trying to poison everything we've built."

The words struck deep, and Pyrrha's heart tightened in her chest. The bond they had once shared so purely now felt like it was being corrupted from within, like a slow, creeping rot eating away at something precious.

The shadows stretched longer, the forest around them darker. As the pair made their way deeper into the unknown, the ever-present feeling of being watched gnawed at their every step. Even the air felt oppressive, thick with something unspoken.

Suddenly, there was a sound. A low, guttural growl that echoed through the trees. Pyrrha froze, her instincts immediately snapping to attention, her sword drawn in an instant.

Aleron's eyes darted around, his hand instinctively resting on the hilt of his own weapon. "We're not alone."

The growl came again, closer this time—louder, more insistent.

"What is that?" Aleron asked, his voice low, cautious.

Before Pyrrha could respond, a figure emerged from the mist, tall and cloaked in dark Armour, a haunting silhouette against the fog. The figure's presence was imposing, as if the very air had grown colder in its wake.

"Who are you?" Pyrrha demanded, her voice steady but laced with suspicion.

The figure raised its head slowly, revealing an unnaturally pale face, its eyes glowing with an eerie, unnatural light. "A messenger," it replied, its voice devoid of emotion. "I bring a warning."

Pyrrha tensed, sensing the danger in its words. "A warning of what?"

The figure's lips twisted into a twisted semblance of a smile. "The bond you share... it is fragile. Do not be fooled into thinking it will be enough to protect you. There are powers beyond your understanding that seek to sever it."

Aleron stepped forward, his hand tightening around his weapon. "What do you want with us?"

The figure's eyes flicked to Aleron, a faint gleam of recognition in them, though it quickly vanished. "Nothing, for now. But understand this: the darkness you fight is not the true enemy. There are forces older than even the darkest shadows you know. Forces that move through time, through minds, through hearts. They will stop at nothing to see you fall."

Before Pyrrha could respond, the figure turned, its cloak billowing like smoke, vanishing into the fog.

"Wait!" Pyrrha called out, but it was too late. The figure had disappeared, leaving behind only the unsettling echo of its words.

Aleron stood beside her, his gaze fixed on the spot where the figure had stood moments ago. "What was that?"

"I don't know," Pyrrha said, her voice tight with tension. "But I don't like the sound of it. What if it is true? What if this darkness—whatever it is—has something even worse waiting for us?"

Aleron placed a hand on her shoulder, grounding her in the present. "Whatever it is, we'll face it together. You and me. We won't let anything tear us apart."

Pyrrha met his gaze, and in that moment, despite the weight of the uncertainty pressing down on them, she found a fleeting comfort in his words.

They continued on through the forest, the shadows now feeling heavier, the whispers of the past beginning to settle in their minds. What lay ahead, they could not know—but they had each other, and for the time being, that would have to be enough.

Chapter Thirteen: The Veil Lifts

The silence of the forest pressed in on them, thick and suffocating. Pyrrha's breath came slower now, each exhale heavy with the weight of their unspoken fears. Despite the strange encounter with the cloaked figure, there was no time to dwell on it—not yet. They had a task to finish, and each step took them deeper into the heart of the unknown.

As they walked, the sun dipped lower in the sky, casting long shadows over the path. The distant echo of the figure's words reverberated in Pyrrha's mind. "The darkness you fight is not the true enemy..."

Her grip on her sword tightened. What could it mean? Had they been fighting the wrong battle all along?

Aleron was silent beside her, his presence a grounding force she could not put into words. Despite the growing tension, despite the looming uncertainty of their future, he was her constant. They had grown stronger together, their bond undeniable. But what if it wasn't enough? What if this new threat was something neither of them could face?

A cold gust of wind swept through the trees, breaking her thoughts. She shivered, pulling her cloak tighter around her shoulders.

"We'll find answers," Aleron said suddenly, his voice low but resolute. "We can't afford to second-guess ourselves now."

Pyrrha nodded, though she was not as certain as he was. They had faced so much, fought so hard to bring peace to the kingdom, but what if the peace they had fought for was just the calm before a far greater storm?

They continued walking, their pace quickening as the darkening forest seemed to close in around them. The faint glow of a distant light flickered ahead—an unnatural glow, one that did not belong to the usual warmth of a campfire or torch.

"Do you see that?" Pyrrha asked, her voice barely above a whisper.

Aleron nodded, his eyes narrowed. "Stay alert."

They approached cautiously, the glow growing brighter the closer they got. As they pushed past a cluster of thick trees, they emerged into a clearing. In the centre, a stone circle stood, ancient and weathered, the edges covered with strange markings. At its heart, a pulsing light shimmered with an ethereal glow, as if it were alive.

"What is this place?" Pyrrha whispered, stepping forward.

"I don't know…" Aleron murmured, his voice tinged with uncertainty. "But something tells me it's important."

Before they could investigate further, the air around them seemed to hum with energy. The light from the stone circle intensified, swirling around them in waves. Pyrrha instinctively stepped back, her hand reaching for her sword, but something held her in place—an unspoken force that made it impossible to move.

Suddenly, the air crackled with a presence, and before them appeared a figure cloaked in shimmering white robes, their face hidden in the folds of the hood. The figure's form was almost translucent, as though they existed between the worlds.

"I've been waiting for you," the figure's voice was calm, but it carried an undeniable weight.

Pyrrha's heart raced. "Who are you?"

The figure stepped forward, their form becoming more solid, the glow of the stones surrounding them flickering as though responding to their presence. "I am the Keeper of the Veil. I guard the passage between realms."

Aleron's brow furrowed. "What is this place? Why have you brought us here?"

The Keeper of the Veil tilted their head, as though considering the question carefully. "This is the threshold—the point where your journey takes a new path. The darkness you have fought is only the surface of something far deeper, far older. It has always existed, waiting."

Pyrrha's pulse quickened. "You mean to say the battle isn't over?"

The Keeper nodded; their expression hidden in shadow. "The battle has only just begun."

Aleron stepped forward, his gaze steady and intense. "What do you want from us?"

The Keeper raised a hand, and in their palm, a single

glowing crystal appeared. "This is the Aetherstone. It is the key to unlocking the truth of the realms, to understanding the true nature of the enemy you face. But it will not come without sacrifice. To wield its power is to risk everything."

Pyrrha and Aleron exchanged a glance. The Aetherstone— it sounded familiar, like something they had heard about long ago in whispers of legend.

"I thought the Aetherstone was a myth," Pyrrha said, her voice betraying the uncertainty she felt.

"It was never a myth," the Keeper replied softly. "It was always real. But only the truly worthy may use it."

"And how do we prove our worth?" Aleron asked, his voice laced with resolve.

The Keeper's lips curved into something resembling a smile, though it was hollow, distant. "You must face the Veil itself. Only then will you understand if you are worthy—or if you are doomed to fail."

With that, the Keeper stepped backward into the light, fading until all that remained was the faint shimmer of the stones and the crystal floating in the air before them.

Pyrrha and Aleron stood in silence, the weight of their new mission settling heavily between them. The path ahead was unclear, but one thing was certain—what they faced was unlike anything they had encountered before.

And the true fight was only just beginning.

Chapter Fourteen: The Trial of the Mind

The air in the cavern grew thick, the scent of ancient stone and magic swirling around them. The Aetherstone pulsed softly between Pyrrha and Aleron, its glow dimming as if it too were anticipating what lay ahead. Ahead of them stood a massive stone door, intricately carved with symbols that seemed to dance and shift when they were not looking directly at them.

Pyrrha's heart pounded in her chest, but she did not need to speak for Aleron to know how she felt. His presence, still new and unfamiliar in the best of ways, soothed her, offering her a silent strength she could never have imagined before their connection.

"I thought the path to the Aetherstone was meant to be straightforward," she whispered, her fingers lightly tracing the edge of the door. The air felt charged, like they were on the cusp of something monumental.

"We both know the Aetherstone never follows a simple path," Aleron replied. His voice was steady, though his eyes searched the door, trying to decipher its riddle. "It's not about finding the easiest way. It is about proving that we're worthy."

He reached out, placing his hand beside hers on the door, and for a moment, they stood in silence, the stone humming in resonance with their connection. The magic was strong, but so was the bond they had forged.

As they touched the stone, the door began to shift, splitting down the middle, revealing an empty void beyond. A swirling mist of silver and blue danced in the air, and a voice, deep and echoing, filled the space.

"Only the truly united may pass. To succeed, your minds must be as one."

Pyrrha glanced at Aleron, a flicker of uncertainty passing through her eyes. "Our minds?"

The voice continued, "You will enter the realm of thought. There, your shared connection will be tested. To succeed, you must solve the riddle of the mind—an answer not just in knowledge, but in understanding."

Aleron squeezed her hand. "We've faced worse."

But even as he said it, he knew this would be different. Their bond had been strong, but this—this would be the ultimate test.

They stepped forward into the mist, and the world around them shifted. One moment, the cavern was gone, replaced by an endless void. Then, a small circle of light appeared, hovering before them.

Inside the circle were images, fleeting but clear: a path, an endless road splitting into three directions, and at the centre, a question:

"Which path leads to the truth?"

As the images blinked, they morphed into something deeper. Each path had a different image associated with

it—one was the familiar sight of their home, the other a sprawling field of endless, twisting vines, and the last—a single, bright star in the distance.

Pyrrha felt Aleron's thoughts fill her mind. We need to trust each other, truly. Think as one. What do you see?

The question felt too simple, but there was weight to it. Their entire future might hinge on the answer, and as the voice from before echoed again, it made their task seem even more impossible.

"You are not just solving a riddle," the voice intoned. "You must decide. The path you choose will not only affect your future, but the future of the realms you've yet to see."

Pyrrha's pulse quickened. Her mind swirled with images and possibilities, the weight of the decision pressing heavily on her chest. What did each path represent? What did it mean to choose?

Then, something shifted within her—a connection with Aleron. He was with her, his thoughts clear, sharp, focused.

The truth is not just in the image we see, Aleron thought. It is in the heart of the decision. The path isn't about knowledge—it's about trust, and the truth we seek isn't always the one we think is easiest to reach.

Pyrrha's eyes widened. He was right. The path with the star—it was not the answer she'd instinctively have chosen. The star was distant, unreachable. It was not about finding something that glittered. It was about the journey.

She closed her eyes, reaching deeper into their connection. The answer lies in the path that requires the most courage, the one that asks us to face uncertainty. The journey is not about certainty—it's about trust, in each other, and in what we cannot yet understand.

Her mind and Aleron's melded seamlessly as they both turned their attention to the path that seemed the least obvious—the twisting, vine-covered road. It was winding, darkened by shadow and shadowed by branches, yet it called to them.

"Together," she whispered aloud.

Aleron nodded. "We choose this path."

The mist swirled and the riddle faded into the air as if it had never been. The path they had chosen materialized before them, the vines parting as if welcoming them. The light from the Aetherstone pulsed once more, brighter than ever, as they stepped forward together.

The Trial of the Mind had tested them, but they had passed, not through knowledge alone, but through the strength of their bond. They knew that their connection was more than just a tool—it was the key to everything.

As they continued down the path, they could feel the power of the Aetherstone growing, the trials ahead still looming, but now, they were ready.

Chapter Fifteen: Trial of the Heart

The sky above them had begun to darken as they ventured deeper into the unknown realm. The air grew thicker, more oppressive, with an energy that felt both ancient and unfamiliar. Pyrrha's hand gripped Aleron's tightly, a silent promise that they were in this together. The further they walked, the more intense the sensation of being watched grew, as if unseen eyes were following their every move.

"I can feel it," Aleron murmured, his voice low. "Something is not right here."

Pyrrha nodded, her senses heightened. "We're not alone."

They passed through a dense thicket of trees, their twisted branches seeming to reach out like skeletal fingers. Ahead, the path opened into a clearing, bathed in an eerie silvery light. In the centre stood a great stone archway, its surface engraved with strange symbols, glowing faintly.

The moment they stepped into the clearing, a powerful force surged through the air, and the ground beneath them trembled. A low, guttural voice echoed from the stone arch.

"Only those who are bound by love and sacrifice can pass this trial. Only the pure of heart may move forward."

Pyrrha and Aleron exchanged a glance, their connection solidifying as they held each other's gaze. The voice continued, rising with an unearthly echo.

"To succeed, you must face the deepest fears and desires of your hearts. Only by overcoming them together can you continue. Fail, and you will remain trapped here forever."

Pyrrha's breath caught in her throat. She could feel the weight of the words pressing down on her. This was no ordinary test. This was a challenge not only of their strength but of their very souls.

Aleron stepped forward, his hand never leaving Pyrrha's. "We will face this together. Our bond is unbreakable."

The ground before them cracked open, and from the darkness, two figures emerged—twins, identical in appearance, but their eyes gleamed with a malevolent light.

"Do you not recognize us?" one of them whispered, her voice cold and familiar. "We are the shadows of your heart, the doubts you've buried deep within. We are everything you fear... and desire."

Pyrrha felt her pulse quicken. These were not strangers. The figures before her were reflections of herself and Aleron—embodiments of their deepest insecurities.

The first figure, a dark reflection of Pyrrha, sneered. "You are weak, Pyrrha. You only fight because you cannot let go of the past. You are driven by vengeance, not by justice. You will never be enough."

The second figure, a twisted reflection of Aleron, grinned cruelly. "And you, Aleron, are nothing more than a prince playing at heroism. You think you are doing what's right, but you only follow Pyrrha because you fear being alone. You will never be worthy of her."

The words cut through the air like a blade, and Pyrrha felt a sudden pang of doubt. Her breath caught in her chest, her mind swirling with insecurities that had always lingered in the back of her thoughts. Was she truly driven by revenge? Did she seek justice, or had she simply become consumed by the need to avenge her father's death?

Aleron's grip on her hand tightened, his voice steady but filled with sorrow. "Do not listen to them, Pyrrha. They are not us. They are the fears we have never faced. We've already overcome these doubts by standing together."

Pyrrha looked into his eyes, seeing the truth in them. The connection they shared, the love they had forged through trials and pain, was unshakable. And in that moment, she realised that it wasn't just their strength that would carry them through—it was their hearts, bound together, stronger than any fear or shadow that sought to tear them apart.

The twin figures before them hissed in frustration. "You think you can defeat us? You think your love can save you?" they spat in unison.

But Pyrrha stepped forward, her voice clear and resolute. "Love is not weakness. It is our strength."

Aleron joined her, his presence a reassuring force. Together, they stood united, their hearts beating as one. "We will face our fears, not run from them."

The twin figures writhed, their forms distorting and shrinking as the light around the clearing intensified. With a final, defiant scream, they dissolved into nothingness.

The air cleared, and the stone archway before them began to glow brighter. The voice from within spoke again, this time softer, almost reverent.

"You have passed the Trial of the Heart. Your bond is true, your love pure. You may continue, united as one."

As the archway parted, a wave of warmth washed over Pyrrha and Aleron. They had conquered yet another challenge—this time, not with brute strength or magic, but with the undeniable truth of their love and connection.

Pyrrha turned to Aleron, her heart swelling with emotion. "We did it. Together."

Aleron's smile was soft, filled with pride and affection. "Always."

Together, they stepped through the archway, ready to face whatever lay ahead. Their bond, forged in trials and strengthened by love, would be their guiding light through the darkness.

Chapter Sixteen: The Beast of the Abyss

The air had changed again. No longer filled with the oppressive weight of darkness, it was now thick with an almost tangible tension, as though the very earth beneath their feet was holding its breath. Pyrrha could feel it in the depths of her soul—something ancient, something primal, was awakening. She glanced at Aleron, his expression serious, his eyes scanning the surroundings.

"This place..." he murmured, "It's as though it's alive."

Pyrrha nodded, her hand instinctively moving to the hilt of her sword. The crystal in her pocket hummed faintly, its presence reminding her of the power she still had yet to fully comprehend. She and Aleron had grown stronger, yes, but they had also discovered the brutal truth: there was a darker force stirring, one that sought to break their connection and destroy everything they held dear.

They pressed forward, deeper into the labyrinth of twisted, jagged rocks. The path was treacherous, winding in impossible directions, as though it had been designed to confuse and lead them astray. Pyrrha could hear strange noises in the distance—low growls, the sound of claws scraping against stone. A shiver ran down her spine.

"I don't like this," she muttered, her voice barely above a whisper.

"We have no choice but to press on," Aleron said, his voice steady, though his eyes betrayed the same unease.

"Whatever it is, we can handle it together."

But just as he spoke, the ground beneath their feet trembled. Pyrrha's heart skipped a beat as a deep roar echoed through the cavern, shaking the very walls. The air grew colder, and the scent of decay and sulphur filled the space around them.

"Something's coming," Pyrrha said, her grip tightening on her sword.

Without warning, a massive shape lunged from the shadows, its glowing red eyes fixed firmly on them. A creature, no, a beast of nightmare—a monstrous wolf-like form, its body covered in black scales, jagged spines running down its back, and its maw dripping with saliva, fangs bared in a menacing snarl.

Its growl shook the air, a deafening, bone-chilling sound that rattled their very souls.

"What in the gods' name is that?" Aleron gasped, his hand instinctively reaching for his sword.

Pyrrha did not hesitate. "The Beast of the Abyss," she said, her voice low and grim. "It's a creature of darkness. We must defeat it before it consumes us."

The beast lunged, but Aleron was faster. He swung his sword in a wide arc, narrowly missing the creature's snapping jaws. Pyrrha rushed forward, her fire-infused blade glowing brighter as she prepared to strike.

But the beast was quicker than she had anticipated. It

dodged her strike and swiped at her with a clawed paw, sending her tumbling backward. The force of the blow left her gasping for breath, her ribs aching from the impact.

"Pyrrha!" Aleron shouted, rushing to her side.

"I'm fine," she grunted, pushing herself up, though her body still trembled from the force of the attack. "We need to be strategic. This creature is fast, but it is not invincible. We need to work together."

Aleron nodded, his face set in determination. "I'll take its attention. You find an opening."

The beast growled again, its red eyes locking onto them both, sensing the bond between them. It let out another deafening roar and lunged forward, aiming for Aleron. He barely managed to raise his sword in time, blocking the beast's claws, but the force sent him skidding back several feet.

"Now!" Pyrrha shouted, her voice sharp with urgency.

She charged, moving swiftly around the creature, her sword dancing through the air. With a quick flick of her wrist, she slashed at the beast's flank, cutting through the scales. The creature yelped in pain but did not back down.

Aleron took the opportunity, his sword flashing as he struck at the beast's vulnerable side. The two of them fought in perfect synchrony, their movements flowing as though they were one. The bond between them had grown stronger than ever before, and their minds, hearts, and actions worked together seamlessly.

But the Beast of the Abyss was relentless. It spun around, its claws swiping in an arc meant to catch both of them. Pyrrha's eyes widened as the claws came toward her, but in that moment, she felt Aleron's presence in her mind, his thoughts clear as if he were right beside her.

Move left, now!

Without hesitation, Pyrrha dodged to the side, narrowly avoiding the creature's lethal swipe. She could feel Aleron's will pushing her forward, his intent guiding her actions, and she responded without a thought.

"Good," Aleron said, his voice resonating through their shared connection. "Now, strike together."

The beast turned, its massive body shifting as it prepared to charge them again. But this time, Pyrrha and Aleron were ready. They stepped in unison, closing the gap between them and the creature, their swords raised. With one final, coordinated strike, they plunged their weapons into the beast's heart.

The Beast of the Abyss let out a final, agonizing roar, its body writhing in agony before it collapsed to the ground, its dark energy dissipating into the air like smoke.

Pyrrha stood, breathing heavily, her sword still glowing from the battle. She glanced at Aleron, who was equally winded but alive, his eyes filled with pride and admiration.

"We did it," she said, a smile tugging at her lips.

Aleron nodded, his hand reaching out to gently take hers. "Together."

As the creature's body disintegrated into nothingness, the tension in the air lifted, and a sense of peace settled over them. But Pyrrha knew that this victory was only temporary. There would be more challenges ahead. More trials to test their bond, their love, and their strength.

But for now, they had won. And that was enough.

Chapter Seventeen: The Mirror of Souls

The calm that followed their victory against the Beast of the Abyss was fleeting. The air around them still carried the scent of battle, but it was different now. There was an unease, a quiet hum beneath the surface of everything, as if the world itself were holding its breath.

Pyrrha stood still, her senses on high alert, trying to understand what had shifted. Aleron was beside her, his hand still gently clasping hers, but even his warmth could not shake the feeling that something was watching them. Waiting.

"Do you feel it?" Pyrrha whispered, her voice tight.

Aleron nodded, his eyes scanning the horizon, the once-calm path now twisting like a living thing. The landscape around them seemed to warp and shift, as though reality itself was bending.

"What is this place?" he murmured, barely above a whisper.

"I don't know," Pyrrha said, her heart pounding in her chest. "But I have a feeling we're about to find out."

As they continued down the jagged path, the ground beneath their feet started to tremble once again, this time in more subtle waves. Their steps became more cautious, as if every stone could be the one that would betray them. The crystal that Pyrrha carried pulsed with an increasing intensity, its energy resonating with the growing tension around them.

Suddenly, the path before them opened into a vast chamber, its walls lined with mirrors—each one tall and dark, their surfaces glinting ominously in the dim light. The mirrors were strange, though, not simply reflecting the surroundings. Each seemed to shimmer with an ethereal glow, showing distorted images of people, places, and scenes that did not belong.

"This is... wrong," Pyrrha said, taking an instinctive step back. "These mirrors—there's something of about them."

Before Aleron could respond, a voice echoed through the chamber, soft and melodic, yet carrying an unmistakable weight of authority.

"Welcome, travellers," the voice sang, its source impossible to pinpoint. "You have entered the Mirror of Souls. A trial awaits. You may leave, if you choose, but know this: none who enter ever do so willingly again."

Pyrrha's breath caught in her throat. The voice was not something she could sense in the physical world, but something deeper. A shadow in her mind. A being that could see their very souls.

"This is it," she said, her eyes narrowing. "The trial of the mind. The trial that separates the worthy from the weak."

Aleron looked at her, his expression hardening. "What does that mean for us?"

"The Mirror of Souls doesn't just show what's in front of you," Pyrrha said quietly, her gaze fixed on the mirrors. "It shows your deepest fears, your hidden desires, your weaknesses. And it forces you to confront them. You may see things... that are not real. Things that will try to break you."

The air thickened as the first mirror in front of them began to shimmer. The glass rippled like water, forming an image: Pyrrha, standing alone in the ruins of her kingdom, the dead bodies of her people scattered at her feet. Her father's body was there too, lifeless, and cold, his crown shattered. She saw herself kneeling beside him, crying, begging for him to return. But it was too late. The kingdom was gone. The people were gone.

"Pyrrha... no," Aleron's voice broke through her vision, his hand on her arm, trying to pull her away from the mirror.

But the image didn't fade. Instead, it grew darker, more intense, until the ground beneath her seemed to split open. Pyrrha reached out, her hands shaking as she tried to hold onto the memory of her father's warmth. But it slipped through her fingers like sand.

"Stop..." she whispered, feeling the weight of grief crushing her chest. She had faced loss before, but this was different. This was not just the death of a loved one. It was the loss of everything she had ever known, the collapse of the very foundation of her existence.

But Aleron was there, his presence solid and grounding. His hand on hers pulled her back, dragging her from the abyss of despair. The vision began to fade, the mirror returning to its original state, but not without leaving an imprint on her heart.

Pyrrha took a deep breath, willing herself to steady. She turned toward Aleron, their shared connection still a beacon in the storm of emotions. She needed him, more than ever.

"Aleron," she whispered, her voice hoarse. "We cannot let this tear us apart. We must hold onto each other. We cannot let our fears control us."

Aleron's gaze softened, and he nodded, his eyes filled with a mixture of sorrow and resolve. "I'm here, Pyrrha. We are not alone in this."

The next mirror shimmered, revealing Aleron's deepest fear. The image was of him, alone, standing in a desolate field, the crown of his kingdom lying shattered at his feet. His people were gone, and his kingdom had crumbled. But this time, his face was filled not with grief, but with shame. He was the one who had failed them. He was the one who had allowed it to happen.

"I..." Aleron's voice faltered. "I couldn't protect them."

"No, Aleron," Pyrrha said softly, stepping closer to him, her heart aching for him. "You cannot carry the weight of everything on your shoulders. No one can. You are not responsible for what happened to your people."

The image wavered, as if the mirror itself were trembling under their words. Slowly, it began to dissipate, but the toll it had taken on Aleron was clear. His expression was tight with the weight of guilt.

"We've faced trials before," he said, his voice hoarse, but determined. "And we will face more. But we will do it together."

The mirrors began to pulse, the reflections distorting and flickering like flames. The next challenge was not just a test of their minds, but a test of their hearts and souls.

"I know," Pyrrha said, squeezing his hand. "Together."

The voices of the mirrors faded, leaving only the distant sound of their breathing and the quiet hum of energy that surrounded them.

But the trial was not over. Not yet.

Chapter Eighteen: The Heart of the Mirror

As the last echoes of the mirror's illusions faded, the chamber around them seemed to shift. The air had grown dense, almost oppressive, as if the walls themselves were closing in, suffocating them with unseen weight. The faint light from the crystals embedded in the chamber's stone walls flickered erratically, casting long, jagged shadows that seemed to dance like living things.

Aleron's grip on Pyrrha's hand tightened as they stood at the centre of the chamber, their minds still reeling from the visions they had witnessed. Each had confronted their greatest fears, their most private regrets. Yet the mirrors had not released them. They lingered, waiting, watching.

"There's something else," Pyrrha whispered, her voice low, as if speaking any louder might summon whatever presence lurked in the shadows. "The trial isn't over."

Aleron nodded, his brow furrowing as he surveyed their surroundings. "The mirrors... they have changed. It's like they are waiting for something."

Before he could finish his thought, the ground beneath them trembled again, more violently this time. The tremors sent cracks spiralling across the floor, and Pyrrha felt the energy in the air thicken, pulling at her, as though something ancient and powerful was stirring.

Then, as suddenly as the tremors had begun, the chamber fell silent. The mirrors, once flickering with distorted images, now seemed perfectly still. But Pyrrha could feel it—the presence that had haunted the room was not gone. It was closer now, as if it had grown bolder, waiting to strike.

"This isn't just about us anymore," she said, her voice steady, but her heart pounding. "The trial has been designed to test more than our minds. It's testing our bond, our unity. If we cannot stand together now, we won't make it through."

Aleron turned to face her, his eyes full of resolve. "We have already made it this far. Whatever happens next, we face it as one. We are not alone in this."

Just as the words left his lips, a low, resonant hum filled the air. It came from all around them, vibrating through the walls and the floor, a sound that seemed to echo within their very souls. The mirrors began to glow with an eerie light, their surfaces swirling as if alive. The images within them distorted and shifted once again, but this time, it was not just the past they revealed. It was the future.

The mirrors showed them a world, dark and twisted, ruled by the very forces they sought to destroy. The kingdoms they fought to protect lay in ruins, their people enslaved by shadow. Pyrrha saw herself standing alone at the edge of a ravaged battlefield, the weight of loss in her eyes. Aleron was there too, his crown shattered, kneeling before an unknown figure—a dark presence that loomed over them, powerful and overwhelming.

"No..." Pyrrha gasped, taking a step back. The images in

the mirrors were too real, too close to what they feared.

Aleron's grip on her hand tightened, his voice filled with urgency. "Pyrrha, it is not real. It's trying to break us."

But Pyrrha could not tear her eyes away. The images, the possibility of failure, were too powerful. She could feel the weight of destiny pressing down on them, the knowledge that their mission could very well end in failure, in the destruction of everything they fought for. The burden was too great.

The mirrors began to shift again, this time focusing on them. The next image was of Pyrrha and Aleron, standing side by side, their hands clasped. But this time, their faces were clouded with doubt. They were not fighting together. Their connection was broken. A chasm opened between them, widening with each passing second.

"Pyrrha..." Aleron's voice cracked as he saw the vision unfold. "Is this... is this what will happen?"

Pyrrha felt her heart lurch. She didn't want to believe it. She couldn't. But the image felt too real, too plausible. She could feel the weight of the prophecy bearing down on her, the knowledge that the greatest threat to their success might be themselves.

"We can't let this happen," she said, her voice trembling, but her resolve sharpening. "We are stronger than this. Together, we are invincible. We have to believe in each other, Aleron. We cannot let fear tear us apart."

Aleron's eyes softened, and he took a deep breath, the

weight of their shared vision settling heavily on his shoulders. He had seen the future they fought to avoid. But even in the face of it, he knew one thing: the strength of their bond was the key to overcoming it.

"I believe in you, Pyrrha," he said quietly. "I believe in us."

The words were simple, but they carried the weight of everything they had endured together. Pyrrha met his gaze, feeling the connection between them grow stronger, the bond deepening as their shared power flowed between them like a current of energy.

Suddenly, the mirrors began to crack, one by one, the images shattering into a thousand pieces. The chamber shook again, but this time it was different. The walls began to bend and warp, as though the very fabric of reality was being torn apart.

In that moment, Pyrrha knew that this trial was not just about overcoming their own fears. It was about protecting what they had built—together. Their love, their bond, their shared purpose—it was the key to defeating the darkness that sought to consume them.

As the last of the mirrors shattered, the chamber collapsed into darkness. But instead of feeling lost, Pyrrha felt a surge of clarity. She and Aleron were not alone. They were bound in a way that nothing—no force, no trial, no enemy—could ever break.

Together, they would face the darkness. Together, they would prevail.

Chapter Nineteen: The Heart of the Storm

The darkness that had once seemed oppressive now felt like a distant memory, though its weight lingered in the back of Pyrrha's mind. She and Aleron stood in the aftermath of the shattered chamber, surrounded by the echoes of the broken mirrors that had once shown them a future of despair. The air was thick with energy, both new and raw, as though the very fabric of reality had been stretched and torn during their trial.

Pyrrha's hand remained clasped tightly in Aleron's, their connection still palpable, the bond forged in the crucible of their shared trials stronger than ever.

The chamber, now devoid of mirrors, had transformed. Where there had once been cold stone walls and jagged reflections, there was now a vast expanse, a swirling vortex of colours and lights that twisted around them like the eye of a storm. A wind, sharp and wild, whipped through the space, carrying with it a chill that seemed to cut straight to their bones.

"We're not alone," Pyrrha murmured, her voice filled with a quiet awe.

Aleron nodded, his eyes scanning the vortex. He, too, could feel it—a presence, powerful and ancient, watching them, waiting. This was not the same trial they had faced before. This was something different, something more primal.

As the storm of light and colour grew more intense, Pyrrha felt the surge of power within her, her connection to Aleron deepening even further. They were no longer just allies. They were something more—two souls bound together, their thoughts intertwined, their magic one. They could hear each other's thoughts without speaking, their minds united in a way that transcended words.

"We have to face this together," Aleron's voice echoed in her mind, steady and clear.

Pyrrha's heart swelled with a fierce determination. She knew now, more than ever, that their bond was their greatest strength. They could overcome anything as long as they remained as one.

A great rumble shook the chamber as a figure began to take form within the swirling vortex. It was a figure cloaked in shadows; its features hidden beneath a hood of darkness. But even without seeing its face, Pyrrha could feel the malice radiating from it, like a dark cloud rolling in over a peaceful sea.

"Who are you?" Pyrrha demanded, her voice ringing out with authority. The figure did not answer, but the air around them grew colder still.

Instead, a voice, low and resonant, echoed through the chamber, reverberating in their very bones.

"You are bound by a connection you do not fully understand. A bond forged in love, yes, but one that is fragile. It will break before long. What happens when the darkness calls, and you no longer have the strength to resist?"

Pyrrha's pulse quickened. The words hit her like a blow, the doubt creeping in again, threatening to break the unity she had worked so hard to build. She glanced at Aleron, his hand still firmly in hers, his eyes locked onto hers with a fierceness that made her heart race.

"Don't listen," Aleron whispered, though his thoughts were filled with a quiet resolve. "This is just another trial, another test. We will face it. Together."

Pyrrha nodded, squeezing his hand. "Together."

The figure before them seemed to smile, though the gesture was more of a distortion in the shadows than anything human. "You think you are prepared. You think you understand the cost of what lies ahead. But do you truly understand what it means to give everything? To sacrifice everything?"

The shadows twisted, and suddenly, Pyrrha and Aleron were no longer standing in the chamber. They were in a darkened forest, the trees twisted and gnarled, their branches clawing at the sky. The air was thick with the scent of decay, and the ground beneath their feet was slick with something dark, as though the earth itself was dying.

"What is this place?" Pyrrha whispered, her heart hammering in her chest.

"This is the future you've seen," the figure's voice

answered, now echoing from all around them. "This is what will happen if you fail. This is what you will lose."

Pyrrha's breath caught in her throat as the vision shifted. Before her stood the ruins of a kingdom, its walls crumbling, its people scattered and broken. Aleron was kneeling in the centre of it all, his crown shattered, blood staining the ground around him. He was alone, and the once-strong kingdom was no more.

She stepped forward, her heart aching at the sight. "No! This can't be…"

"You cannot save them all," the figure warned, its voice like a hiss. "The cost of victory is more than you realise. What will you sacrifice? Will you give up your love for the greater good? Will you sacrifice him?"

The words struck her like a dagger to the chest. She felt herself falter; the weight of the choice she might one day have to make pressing down on her. The images shifted again, and now it was Aleron standing before her, his face twisted with sorrow.

"Pyrrha," his voice, weak and strained, echoed through the vision. "I'm sorry. I can't do this. I can't be what you need me to be."

The words tore through her heart, and for a moment, she could feel the doubt creeping in, threatening to consume her.

But then, a steady presence in her mind pushed it all away. It was Aleron, his thoughts merging with hers, his resolve solidifying in the face of the storm.

"Pyrrha, I need you to hear me," his voice whispered in her mind. "You are not alone. We are not alone. Our bond is stronger than this. Together, we can face anything."

The vision began to crack, the darkness flickering, revealing the truth hidden beneath the shadows. Pyrrha closed her eyes, focusing on the warmth of Aleron's thoughts in her mind, the strength of his presence, and the love they shared. She felt his love for her, and in turn, she poured her heart into him, sharing everything—her fear, her hope, her love, her resolve.

When she opened her eyes again, the vision was gone. The dark forest faded, the ruined kingdom vanished, and the figure before them had dissipated into smoke.

"Together," Pyrrha whispered, her voice steady, her heart unshakable. "We are stronger than this."

Aleron stepped closer, his hand finding hers again. Their bond, their connection, was unbreakable now. Whatever trials lay ahead, they would face them side by side.

"Together," Aleron repeated, his voice filled with quiet strength. "Always."

Chapter Twenty: Secrets of the Forgotten Ones

The swirling vortex of light and shadow faded, leaving Pyrrha and Aleron standing in the silent chamber once more. The echoes of the trial still lingered in their minds—the doubts, the visions of a shattered future. But now, something had changed. Their bond had grown even stronger, their unity unshaken despite the forces that had tried to drive them apart.

A deep hum resonated through the air, low and vibrating, as if the very walls of the temple were alive. Aleron turned to Pyrrha, his golden eyes reflecting the strange glow that now pulsed from the centre of the room.

"The presence that tested us," Aleron murmured, "it wasn't just some illusion. It was ancient, something beyond even the dark sorcerers we have faced."

Pyrrha nodded, gripping the hilt of her sword. "It spoke as if it knew the cost of our quest. As if it had seen others try and fail."

The air shimmered, and suddenly, a massive circular engraving in the floor began to glow with radiant energy. Runes, older than any Pyrrha had seen before, pulsed with shifting patterns of gold and deep violet. From the centre of the circle, a figure began to form—ethereal, wrapped in flowing robes of stardust and shadow.

A voice, layered with centuries of wisdom and sorrow, spoke.

"You have passed the first trial. But understanding comes only to those willing to seek beyond what is seen."

Pyrrha instinctively took a step forward, her body tense but ready. "Who are you?"

The figure did not move but seemed to watch them with unseen eyes. "We are the Forgotten Ones, the keepers of the balance between light and dark. Long ago, we stood where you now stand. We, too, sought to wield power beyond our understanding. And we, too, thought love alone could defy the tides of fate."

A chill ran down Pyrrha's spine. "What happened?"

The figure's presence darkened, as though grief itself had settled around it. "We failed. And because of that failure, the darkness grew stronger. The cycle of war and ruin continued. The very thing we fought against consumed us."

Aleron's jaw tightened. "Then why test us? If we are doomed to fail, what purpose does this trial serve?"

"Because we wish to see if you will break the cycle. If you will learn what we could not."

The chamber trembled as the figure raised an ethereal hand, and suddenly, the walls around them vanished, replaced by a vast, cosmic expanse. Stars burned in the distance, swirling around them in patterns that felt both ancient and alive. In the centre of this celestial void, a great balance scale appeared, one side glowing with golden light, the other with endless shadow.

"The forces you fight are not just evil. They are part of a greater balance. Light cannot exist without shadow, nor can shadow without light. But there are those who wish to tip the scales forever, to drown the world in one or the other. That is the battle you now fight."

Pyrrha clenched her fists. "And how do we win?"

The figure extended its hands, and between its palms, two glowing symbols appeared—one a radiant flame, the other a dark crescent. "You have wielded fire, Pyrrha Infernal. You have wielded the strength of righteous fury. And you, Aleron, have wielded wisdom, control, and restraint. But power alone will not be enough."

Aleron stepped forward. "Then what will be enough?"

The celestial figure turned its gaze upon him. "Understanding. The magic you seek to destroy is not merely darkness—it is imbalance. To defeat it, you must not only fight against it but learn its nature. You must understand how it works, how it consumes, and how it is undone."

Pyrrha exchanged a look with Aleron. This was not what she had expected. She had thought their journey was to destroy dark magic, to purge it from the world. But now, the truth was shifting before her eyes.

"There is a place where this knowledge lies hidden," the figure continued. "A temple lost to time, buried deep within the Valley of Echoes. There, the knowledge of the first wielders remains. But beware, for the valley does not give up its secrets freely. If you go, you must be prepared for the truth you may uncover."

The vision of the celestial balance flickered and began to fade. The figure's form grew dim, its energy retreating back into the runes on the floor.

"Your true trial is yet to come. Seek the Temple of the First Flame, and there, you may find the answers you need."

With those final words, the chamber returned to normal, the runes dimming, the walls solidifying once more. The silence that followed was heavy with meaning.

Pyrrha exhaled slowly, her heart pounding. She looked at Aleron, and in his gaze, she saw the same determination that burned within her.

"The Valley of Echoes," Aleron murmured. "A place spoken of only in myths."

Pyrrha sheathed her sword. "Then it's time we turned myth into reality."

With that, they turned toward the temple's exit, stepping forward into the unknown once more—toward a valley lost to time, and the truth that waited within.

Chapter Twenty-One: The Valley of Echoes

The journey to the Valley of Echoes was unlike any Pyrrha and Aleron had ever faced. The land itself seemed forsaken, untouched by time yet burdened with ancient sorrow. Towering cliffs, jagged and lifeless, loomed on either side of the narrow path they followed. The air was thick, humming with an eerie energy—whispers that had no source, shadows that moved without cause.

The valley was not merely a place. It was alive, watching, waiting.

Pyrrha tightened her grip on her sword's hilt. "I can feel it," she murmured. "This place… it's as if the past itself lingers here."

Aleron walked beside her, his gaze scanning the surroundings. "The spirits of those who came before." He exhaled. "The Forgotten Ones warned us—this valley does not give up its secrets freely."

A gust of wind howled through the narrow ravine, carrying with it faint, unintelligible voices. It was as if the very air whispered memories of those who had perished here.

Then, suddenly, the path ahead of them shifted.

One moment, it was solid ground—dusty stone beneath their boots. The next, it twisted, distorting into something unnatural. The valley seemed to stretch impossibly far, as if time and space had unravelled. Pyrrha took a step onward but immediately recoiled. The ground beneath her shimmered like water, a mirage of shifting colours.

"We're being tested," Aleron said grimly. "The valley is warping reality around us."

Pyrrha nodded. "Then we find the truth hidden within the illusion."

She closed her eyes, focusing not on what she saw, but on what she felt. The bond between her and Aleron had deepened beyond words, beyond even thought. She reached out through that connection, allowing their unity to guide them.

And then—she felt it.

A crack in the illusion. A thread of truth woven into the falsehood.

"There." Pyrrha's eyes snapped open. She pointed ahead, toward a jagged archway that flickered between existence and nothingness. "It is real. The rest is a trap."

Aleron followed her lead without question. As they stepped forward, the distorted landscape fought against them, but their bond burned like a beacon in the dark. Together, they pushed through the false reality until the world around them snapped back into place.

The mirage vanished, revealing a true path—a hidden passage descending into the heart of the valley.

Aleron exhaled. "That was only the first layer of deception."

Pyrrha nodded. "And I doubt it will be the last."

They pressed onward, deeper into the valley where even greater truths—and greater dangers—awaited.

Chapter Twenty-Two: Shadows of the Past

Descending into the valley's depths, Pyrrha and Aleron felt the weight of unseen eyes pressing upon them. The walls of the ravine pulsed with energy, as if the very stone was breathing, listening. The whispers that had once been distant now grew clearer, forming half-spoken words that brushed against their minds.

"You seek knowledge... but will you bear its cost?"

The voice was neither male nor female, neither young nor old. It was a chorus of many, layered upon each other, woven into the very air.

Pyrrha stilled, her hand instinctively tightening around her sword's hilt. "Do you hear that?"

Aleron nodded. "It's speaking directly into our thoughts."

A cold mist coiled around their feet, rising like fingers grasping at their ankles. Then, without warning, the mist thickened and took shape. Figures emerged—transparent at first, then more defined. Warriors clad in battle-worn armour, eyes hollow, swords clutched in lifeless hands.

Pyrrha's breath caught in her throat. "They're... echoes."

One stepped forward, his Armour dented, his once-proud crest stained with the passage of time. "You walk the path of kings and conquerors," he intoned, his voice carrying the weight of centuries. "But power alone is not enough. You must face the truth that binds you."

Before Pyrrha could speak, the warriors raised their swords—and the valley became a battlefield.

Blades clashed against unseen foes. The warriors fought shadows that took no form, yet every swing seemed desperate, every motion an endless struggle.

Aleron took a step forward. "They're trapped," he realised. "This isn't just a test. This is their torment."

Pyrrha's eyes widened as recognition struck her. "These are the ones who failed before us."

The spirits turned their hollow gazes upon them.

"Will you share our fate?"

The mist surged forward, wrapping around Pyrrha and Aleron, pulling them into the battle—not with swords, but with their minds. Images flashed before them—visions of past warriors who had stood where they now stood, each seeking knowledge, each falling to the valley's illusions.

Pyrrha clenched her fists, pushing back against the invading presence. She felt Aleron beside her, their connection flickering like a flame against the storm.

"No," she said firmly. "We are not like those before us."

She reached for Aleron's hand. The moment their fingers met, their bond ignited—light bursting from within them, scattering the mist.

The spirits recoiled. The battlefield wavered. The illusions cracked like glass. A single figure remained. Unlike the others, he did not wield a blade. He wore robes of silver and deep violet, his face half-hidden by the shadows of a hood. He studied them, his eyes sharp and knowing.

"You have come far," he said, his voice no longer an echo. "But the valley is not yet done with you."

With a wave of his hand, the mist swirled again—and the world around them shifted once more.

Darkness consumed the valley, and Pyrrha and Aleron found themselves standing in an unfamiliar place—where the greatest trial yet awaited.

Chapter Twenty-Three: The Trial of Truth

The darkness pressed in, thick and suffocating, as if the valley itself had swallowed them whole. Pyrrha and Aleron stood motionless, gripping each other's hands, their bond the only anchor against the abyss.

Then, like a star igniting in the void, a single light flared ahead—a silver flame, flickering in the distance. The robed figure stood beside it, his hood casting deeper shadows over his face.

"This is your final trial," he intoned. "One that no warrior's blade can overcome."

Pyrrha narrowed her eyes. "What must we do?"

The figure raised his hands. The darkness around them rippled, shifting like water, and suddenly, the void was no longer empty. Reflections appeared... mirrors of Pyrrha and Aleron, but distorted, fractured, twisted by something unseen.

Pyrrha gasped. Her own reflection sneered back at her, eyes burning with fury, her flaming sword clutched in her hand. But there was something... wrong. The fire was wild, unchecked, engulfing her entire form like a raging inferno.

The reflection's voice was sharp as a dagger. "Justice?" it mocked. "No, you seek revenge. You crave destruction. You would burn the world to satisfy your grief."

Aleron turned sharply as his own reflection stepped

forward—a shadowy figure clad in royal armour, a dark crown upon his head. The figure smirked. "You claim to stand for righteousness, but do you not long for power? A kingdom of your own? The right to rule, to shape the world as you see fit?"

The words struck deep, slithering into their minds like poison.

"No." Pyrrha clenched her fists, trying to ignore the burning in her chest. "That's not who I am."

The reflection laughed coldly. "Are you certain? Do you not feel it—how easy it would be to give in? To strike down your enemies without mercy? To take what is rightfully yours?"

Aleron's jaw tightened. "We do not fight for ourselves."

The shadow of himself tilted its head. "Then why hesitate? Why doubt? If you are truly righteous, why does fear still grip your heart?"

The flames of the silver torch flickered wildly, the space around them trembling under the weight of their choices.

Pyrrha swallowed hard. She could feel it—that tiny ember inside her, the temptation to let rage guide her sword. She had buried it beneath duty and honour, but here, in this valley, there was no hiding.

She turned to Aleron, her voice soft but steady. "We have to accept it."

Aleron's eyes met hers, his mind racing. "Accept what?"

"That we could become them." Her breath hitched, but she forced the words out. "That the darkness exists inside us. That we have the power to fall."

His grip on her hand tightened.

The trial was not about rejecting the darkness. It was about facing it. Acknowledging that it lived within them—but choosing to rise above it.

Pyrrha inhaled deeply, standing tall. "I will not deny my anger." She met her reflection's burning gaze. "But I will not let it control me."

Aleron followed her lead, squaring his shoulders. "I could take power—but I choose not to."

Their reflections flickered. The twisted images wavered, cracking like broken glass. The valley trembled. The silver flame surged.

Then—silence.

The robed figure stepped forward, his expression unreadable. "You have passed."

Pyrrha exhaled shakily. The weight that had pressed on her chest lifted.

Aleron looked to the figure. "What was this trial meant to teach us?"

The man's gaze softened. "That true strength is not found in battle, nor in magic. It is found in choice." He gestured to the torch. "The fire of truth only burns for those who see themselves clearly."

Pyrrha and Aleron exchanged a glance. They had come to this valley seeking knowledge—but they had found something greater.

The silver fire rose, surrounding them in a warm, cleansing light. The valley, once shrouded in darkness, began to fade.

And as the light took them, they knew—they were no longer the same warriors who had entered.

Chapter Twenty-Four: The Burden of Knowledge

The silver light faded, leaving Pyrrha and Aleron standing once more in the ancient temple chamber. The robed figure was gone, and the valley of darkness had vanished as if it had never existed.

Yet, the weight of what they had seen still clung to them.

Pyrrha clenched her fists. The reflection of herself—twisted, consumed by fury—still lingered in her mind. She had faced it, accepted it, but that did not mean the darkness was gone.

Aleron turned to her, his expression unreadable. "You felt it too, didn't you?"

She nodded slowly. "Yes. The temptation. The hunger for revenge."

He exhaled. "And I felt the thirst for power." His gaze darkened. "It was intoxicating."

Pyrrha looked at him, sensing the unease in his voice. She reached for his hand, intertwining her fingers with his. "But we overcame it. We chose differently."

Aleron's grip tightened. "For now."

Before Pyrrha could answer, a deep rumble echoed through the chamber. The ground beneath them trembled. From the altar at the temple's heart, a brilliant white flame ignited, swirling upward in a pillar of light.

The flames twisted and parted, revealing a figure within.

She was tall, ethereal, her form barely tangible, like a memory given shape. Her long robes shimmered with the light of the stars, and her eyes—deep and ancient—held the weight of eternity.

"Who are you?" Pyrrha asked, stepping forward cautiously.

The woman's voice was both a whisper and a roar. "I am the Guardian of the Eternal Flame."

Aleron swallowed. "And why have you revealed yourself to us?"

The Guardian studied them. "Because you have passed the Trial of Truth. Few ever do." Her gaze softened. "You have seen what lies within, and still, you walk forward. That is rare."

Pyrrha hesitated. "Then tell us… what is it we seek?"

The Guardian raised her hands, and the flames around her pulsed. "You came searching for knowledge. You wished to understand the ancient forces that oppose you."

Aleron nodded. "Yes. The darkness we face is growing stronger. We must know how to fight it."

The Guardian sighed. "There is no single weapon against darkness. No spell, no blade, no power that will ever truly vanquish it."

Pyrrha frowned. "Then how do we win?"

The Guardian met her gaze. "You do not 'win.' You endure."

The words settled heavily between them.

Aleron's jaw tightened. "Then why bring us here? Why test us?"

The Guardian stepped forward, the flames parting around her like water. "Because knowledge is power. And power is a burden. You are not here to destroy the darkness. You are here to balance it."

Pyrrha's heart pounded. "Balance?"

The Guardian nodded. "The world has always been light and shadow. One cannot exist without the other. Too much light, and all is consumed in purity. Too much darkness, and all is lost to oblivion."

Aleron's eyes narrowed. "You're saying we have to let darkness exist?"

The Guardian sighed. "I am saying you must understand it. Respect it. Only by knowing its nature can you prevent it from consuming everything."

Pyrrha felt a shiver crawl up her spine. "But we have seen what darkness does. It kills. It corrupts."

The Guardian inclined her head. "Yes. And yet, you, Pyrrha, have darkness within you, do you not?"

Pyrrha froze.

Aleron stepped closer to her protectively. "That's not the same."

The Guardian's gaze softened. "Isn't it? You felt the rage, the hunger for vengeance. You felt the fire inside you, calling for destruction."

Pyrrha swallowed hard. "I did."

The Guardian turned to Aleron. "And you, prince, felt the desire for control. The longing for power."

Aleron's fists clenched. "Yes."

The Guardian gestured between them. "And yet, here you stand. You did not succumb. That is the balance."

The chamber fell silent.

Pyrrha exhaled slowly. "So, what do we do?"

The Guardian studied them for a long moment. Then, she raised her hand, and between her fingers, a single flame flickered—gold and black, twisting together in harmony.

"You must learn to wield both," she said.

Aleron tensed. "Dark magic?"

The Guardian's expression was unreadable. "Not dark magic. But understanding. Strength comes from knowledge, and the only way to truly fight the enemy is to know them."

Pyrrha's thoughts raced. The very idea went against everything she had believed. And yet... the words rang with truth.

The Guardian reached out, and the flame floated toward

them. It hovered between Pyrrha and Aleron, pulsing gently.

"This is the first step," the Guardian said. "Will you take it?"

Pyrrha met Aleron's gaze. He searched her face, and in that moment, they understood each other completely.

She turned back to the Guardian. "Yes."

As the flame touched their hands, warmth flooded through them. A rush of understanding, of power, of something neither of them had ever felt before.

The path ahead was uncertain. But together, they would walk it.

Chapter Twenty-Five: Awakening the Twin Flame

The moment the flame touched their hands, Pyrrha and Aleron gasped. A surge of heat—both comforting and overwhelming—coursed through them, binding their souls even tighter than before. It was not just power, but understanding, an ancient force neither had ever known.

Pyrrha's vision blurred, and for a moment, she saw not just herself but Aleron—as if she were inside his mind. She felt his thoughts, his fears, his hopes. And she knew, without doubt, that he could feel hers.

Aleron stiffened, his grip on her tightening. "Pyrrha… I can hear you."

Pyrrha's breath caught. "And I can hear you."

The Guardian watched with solemn eyes. "You have awakened the Twin Flame—the bond that few in this world ever attain. It is not just a connection of love, but of soul and spirit. You are one."

Pyrrha could barely breathe. It was unlike anything she had ever experienced. She had always trusted Aleron, had always felt his presence, but now… now they were each other.

Aleron turned to the Guardian. "What does this mean?"

The Guardian stepped forward. "It means you are no longer separate. Your minds, your hearts, your strength—it is shared. You will feel each other's pain, each other's joy. And in battle, you will fight as one."

Pyrrha's fingers tightened around Aleron's. The implications were both exhilarating and terrifying. If one of them was wounded, would the other feel it? If one fell... would the other?

The Guardian must have sensed her thoughts, for she spoke gently. "This bond is powerful, but it is also a burden. It will strengthen you beyond anything you have ever known. But if you are not careful, it will also become your greatest weakness."

Aleron's gaze darkened. "Because if one of us is lost, the other will never be whole again."

The Guardian nodded. "Yes. And if either of you falters, the balance between you may shatter."

Pyrrha inhaled deeply, steadying herself. "Then we must never falter."

Aleron turned to her, his expression firm yet filled with something deeper—something unbreakable. "We won't."

The Guardian studied them for a long moment before nodding. "Then your journey continues. But be warned— now that you have awakened the Twin Flame, others will sense it. The darkness will seek to corrupt it. And those who fear such power... will try to destroy it."

Pyrrha squared her shoulders. "Let them try."

Aleron smirked. "We're ready."

The Guardian gave them a knowing look. "We shall see."

With that, she lifted her hands, and the temple chamber around them began to dissolve into shimmering light.

Pyrrha barely had time to blink before the world shifted, and they were somewhere else entirely.

Their true test had only just begun.

Chapter Twenty-Six: The First Trial

The world around them solidified into a vast, open expanse. Towering monolithic stones jutted from the earth; their surfaces etched with ancient runes that glowed faintly under the ethereal sky. A cold wind howled through the empty space, whispering secrets lost to time.

Pyrrha shivered, gripping Aleron's hand. "Where are we?"

Aleron scanned the surroundings. "It feels… ancient. Like something has been waiting here for centuries."

A voice, deep and commanding, echoed through the void.

"You who have awakened the Twin Flame… prove your unity or be undone."

A shudder ran down Pyrrha's spine. She instinctively tightened her grip on Aleron, feeling his pulse align with hers.

A shadow materialized before them—a dark silhouette with burning violet eyes. It had no distinct form, shifting like living smoke, but its presence was suffocating.

"This is the Trial of Division," the shadow intoned. "You claim to be one, but can you endure being torn apart?"

The instant the words were spoken, an invisible force struck them both. Pyrrha gasped as she felt herself being pulled away from Aleron. She reached for him, but an

unseen barrier had formed between them, a wall of

shimmering energy that no blade could pierce.

"Aleron!" she shouted.

"I'm here!" His voice was distant, as if he were on the other side of a great chasm. He slammed his fists against the barrier, but it did not yield.

The shadow shifted; its gaze fixed on Pyrrha. "A soul divided cannot stand. Can you survive without feeling his presence? Without hearing his thoughts? Without knowing he is there?"

The moment the words left the shadow's mouth, the bond between them—so strong, so unbreakable—was severed.

Pyrrha gasped, staggering backward as a deep, hollow emptiness filled her. It was as if part of her soul had been torn away, leaving her cold and disoriented. She reached out mentally, searching for Aleron's presence... but he was gone.

No. Not gone. Just... unreachable.

She clenched her fists, forcing herself to steady her breathing. This was the trial. This was what the darkness feared—that together, they were unstoppable.

So, the test was simple: force them apart and see if they would crumble.

"You are nothing without him," the shadow whispered.

Pyrrha's eyes narrowed. "That's where you're wrong."

With a battle cry, she drew her sword, its flames roaring to life, illuminating the darkness. The shadow recoiled slightly but did not flee.

She didn't need to feel Aleron to know he was fighting, just as she was. Their bond was not built on proximity—it was built on trust, on love, on an unshakable belief that no force in existence could break them.

No matter how far they were torn apart, they would always find their way back to each other.

A deep pulse of energy surged through her, and in an instant, she felt him again—faint, but there. Aleron.

And he was fighting too.

The shadow hissed. "Impossible."

Pyrrha smirked. "You don't know us very well, do you?"

The Trial of Division had begun, but it would not end the way the darkness intended.

The void collapsed around them. The battlefield of illusions, of division and deception, faded into nothingness. For a brief moment, Pyrrha and Aleron were suspended in an abyss of weightless silence. Then—

The world reformed.

Chapter Twenty-Seven: The Trial of Devotion

They stood together in a vast, ancient hall. Towering pillars, engraved with celestial symbols, reached toward an unseen sky. A soft, golden light filtered down from above, casting a glow upon the polished marble floor beneath their feet. A grand doorway lay ahead, massive and imposing, its surface carved with intricate patterns that seemed to shift and breathe.

Pyrrha's grip tightened on her sword. She had learned by now that nothing here was as it seemed. "What now?" she murmured.

Aleron stepped beside her. "The Trial of Devotion," he said, voice steady but wary. "That's what the Ancients called it."

She turned to him. "Devotion to what?"

Before he could answer, a voice echoed through the chamber—a deep, resonant tone that carried the weight of ages.

"Devotion is the foundation upon which all true power is built."

From the shadows, three figures emerged.

Pyrrha tensed, her instincts screaming of danger. The figures were cloaked in flowing, ethereal robes, their faces hidden behind ornate masks. But it was the energy radiating from them that sent a shiver down her spine. It was as if the very air bowed to their presence.

One of them stepped forward. "You have proven your unity of mind. But devotion is not merely thought—it is action. It is sacrifice."

Another voice joined. "One of you must step forward. One of you must choose."

Aleron exhaled sharply. "Choose what?"

The third figure raised a hand.

Between them, the floor shimmered, and a pedestal rose. Upon it lay two identical golden daggers, their blades gleaming like liquid fire.

Pyrrha's pulse quickened. She did not like where this was going.

"The blade in your hands," the first figure intoned, "will test the depth of your devotion."

Pyrrha glanced at Aleron. His jaw was tight, his expression unreadable, but she could feel the tension radiating from him.

"Devotion is more than love," the second figure continued. "It is the willingness to endure pain, to make choices that cost. Only through such trials is true power forged."

Aleron moved first. Without hesitation, he strode to the pedestal, taking one of the daggers in his hand.

The air trembled.

Pyrrha's breath caught. She did not know what was about to happen, but everything in her soul told her this was dangerous.

The robed figures gestured toward her. "Will you take up the blade, warrior princess? Or will you let your beloved stand alone?"

There was no choice.

Pyrrha stepped forward and took the second dagger.

The moment her fingers closed around the hilt; the world changed again.

Pain.

It struck like a bolt of lightning through her soul, searing, burning, unravelling. Pyrrha fell to her knees, her vision blurring as an unbearable weight pressed upon her heart. She felt Aleron's pain—not just his physical agony, but his emotions, his fears, his burdens.

She gasped as memories flooded into her mind.

Aleron as a child, standing alone in a cold palace, his father's harsh words cutting deeper than any blade.

Aleron in battle, forcing himself to remain strong when his men fell around him.

Aleron watching her walk away, when he had not yet been able to tell her the truth of who he was.

The weight of his love for her, his determination, his silent struggles—she felt them all as though they were her own.

Through the haze of suffering, she turned her head and

saw him—

Aleron knelt across from her, his hands clenched into fists, his body trembling. His face was pale with strain, his eyes filled with something raw and unguarded.

Because he was feeling her pain.

Her grief.

Her rage at the injustice of her father's death.

Her moments of doubt when she had wondered if she was strong enough.

Her quiet fear that she would fail, that she would lose everything before she could set things right.

The burden she had never let herself share with anyone— he bore it now, as she bore his.

Pyrrha's heart pounded. This was not an illusion. This was real.

They had become one in mind before, but now... now they were one in soul.

She didn't fight the pain.

She accepted it.

She let herself feel him—every scar, every wound, every struggle. And in doing so, she gave herself to him.

Aleron's breath shuddered. His golden eyes met hers, and in that instant, something shifted between them.

A force unlike anything they had known surged through them both.

The pain did not disappear—but it transformed.

It became power.

The robed figures watched in silence as the light around Pyrrha and Aleron burned brighter, a golden radiance that pulsed in time with their heartbeats.

The first figure spoke at last. "You have chosen to bear each other's burdens. To suffer together. To rise together."

The daggers in their hands dissolved into pure light, flowing into their chests.

Pyrrha gasped as warmth flooded her, the last remnants of pain vanishing.

Aleron stood, reaching a hand to her. She took it without hesitation.

The trial was over.

And they had emerged stronger than ever.

Chapter Twenty-Eight: The Final Trial

The chamber dissolved around them. The golden light faded, and the ancient hall fell away into a vast, star-strewn void. Pyrrha and Aleron stood side by side, their hands still entwined, the weight of the last trial settling deep into their souls.

They had shared pain. They had seen the raw depths of each other's burdens. And through it, their bond had solidified into something unbreakable.

But the test was not yet over.

A new presence stirred in the darkness ahead.

From the shadows, a colossal form emerged—neither beast nor man, but something beyond mortal comprehension. Its towering silhouette flickered between shapes—sometimes a knight in gleaming black armour, sometimes a monstrous, fanged entity, and sometimes... a swirling storm of darkness itself.

Then, it spoke.

"You have proven your unity of mind. You have proven your devotion in soul. But will you prove your will to stand as one—when all is torn apart?"

The words shivered through the void; a challenge wrapped in a promise of suffering.

Pyrrha drew her sword, its flames flaring in defiance.

Aleron summoned his own blade, its silver edge glowing with quiet power.

"What is this trial?" Pyrrha demanded.

The entity's shifting form steadied. It took the shape of a towering warrior clad in obsidian armour, a massive sword of shadow forming in its grip. Its voice was calm, yet merciless.

"The Trial of Separation."

Before they could react, a blinding force erupted between them.

Pyrrha felt her hand ripped from Aleron's. A wave of power threw her backward, tumbling her into an abyss of whirling darkness. She cried out, reaching for him—but he was already gone.

She landed hard on solid ground.

But she was alone.

Pyrrha scrambled to her feet, her heart pounding. She stood in an empty battlefield, grey and lifeless. The silence pressed in around her, suffocating.

No sign of Aleron. No sign of the entity.

Just her.

Alone.

No.

She gritted her teeth, gripping her sword. "Aleron!" she shouted, but her voice barely carried in the dead air.

No answer.

Her mind reached for their bond—the connection they had just forged through pain and devotion.

Nothing.

The emptiness hit her like a dagger to the chest.

Panic clawed at her. Was this the trial? To be truly severed from him?

She had fought alone before. She had suffered alone before. But after everything they had just endured, after feeling his very soul—to be without him now felt like a wound that bled unseen.

She took a breath. Steady.

She would not fail.

She would find him.

Lifting her sword, she took her first step forward—

And the battlefield changed.

A whisper filled the air.

"Why do you fight, Pyrrha?"

She froze.

The voice was unmistakable. It was one she had longed to

hear for so long—one she had feared she would never hear again.

Her father.

Her throat tightened as she turned. And there he was.

The King stood before her, just as she remembered him— the same kind, wise eyes, the same proud bearing. His Armour gleamed, and his royal cloak drifted in an unseen wind.

"Father…" she breathed.

But something was wrong.

His expression was not warm. His eyes were not gentle.

He looked at her with quiet disappointment.

"You chase justice," he said. "But what have you truly accomplished?"

A cold weight settled in Pyrrha's chest. "I've fought for the truth," she said firmly. "I will not stop until I avenge you."

Her father shook his head. "Avenge me?" His gaze turned piercing. "Or destroy yourself?"

Pyrrha flinched.

"No…" she whispered.

The King took a step closer. "You have bound yourself to another. You claim to stand together. But when darkness

comes—when all crumbles—can you honestly say you will

not falter?"

Pyrrha felt the weight of his words settle deep in her bones.

And then—his form shifted.

The King was gone.

In his place stood Aleron.

But not the Aleron she knew.

His golden eyes were dim, his face cold. His blade was drawn, its silver edge gleaming with unfamiliar menace.

"Pyrrha," he said, voice empty. "You do not need me. You never did."

She staggered back. "What...?"

"You are stronger alone," he continued. "You always have been. What if I was only a burden? What if I only made you weaker?"

Her chest tightened.

This is not real.

But the doubt clawed at her, relentless and cruel.

What if she was making a mistake? What if relying on him—needing him—was the weakness that would break them both?

Aleron lifted his blade. "You should let me go."

Pyrrha's grip on her sword trembled.

Then—

She felt something.

A whisper in the back of her mind. A warmth, small but steady.

Pyrrha…

Her heart clenched.

Chapter Twenty-Nine: The Trial Continues

It was him. The real Aleron.

Somewhere, beyond this illusion, beyond this trial—he was reaching for her.

Her fingers tightened around her sword. Her voice was a whisper but filled with unwavering certainty.

"No."

The false Aleron hesitated.

Pyrrha raised her blade, her eyes blazing with fury and love. "You are not real," she said. "And I will not let you take what we have built."

The illusion flickered.

The battlefield shuddered.

A wave of light exploded outward from her, tearing through the false vision.

And then—

She saw him.

Aleron, standing across the void, battling his own illusions. His blade was drawn, his eyes searching—

Until they found her.

The moment their gazes locked, their connection reignited.

The trial's power tried to hold them apart, but they reached for each other anyway.

Aleron moved first, sprinting toward her. Pyrrha ran to meet him.

The force between them shattered—

And then, they were together.

Aleron's arms wrapped around her, and she clung to him, her breath ragged. The overwhelming sense of loss, of doubt, of fear—it was gone.

Because they were one again.

The void trembled. The robed figures reappeared.

The first one spoke, a note of reverence in their voice.

"You have conquered the final trial. You have proven your bond cannot be severed."

A golden doorway rose before them, gleaming with power.

"The knowledge you seek lies beyond this gate. Go forth— together."

Pyrrha and Aleron exchanged a glance. They did not need to speak.

Hand in hand, they stepped through.

Chapter Thirty: The Secrets of the Temple

As Pyrrha and Aleron stepped through the golden doorway, a brilliant light enveloped them. The sensation was unlike anything they had ever felt—neither warmth nor cold, neither weight nor weightlessness. It was as if they were passing through the essence of time itself.

Then, the light faded, and they emerged into a vast, circular chamber unlike any they had seen before.

The walls shimmered with inscriptions, ancient symbols glowing with ethereal blue light. The ceiling stretched impossibly high, a dome of pure crystal reflecting countless constellations—stars that shifted and pulsed as though alive. In the centre of the chamber stood an altar of smooth obsidian, upon which rested a single object: a crystal, pulsating with an otherworldly radiance.

Pyrrha's breath caught. She had seen many wonders, but this—this was something beyond the mortal realm. She felt the weight of centuries pressing upon her, as if the air itself carried the whispers of those who had come before.

Aleron, his hand still firmly clasping hers, took a cautious step forward. "Is this what we seek?"

Before Pyrrha could answer, a voice echoed through the chamber—deep, resonant, neither male nor female but something ancient and eternal.

"You who have braved the trials, who have proven the

strength of your bond, stand before the Heart of Aether."

A ghostly figure emerged from the shadows of the chamber. Cloaked in flowing robes of silver and gold, its face was obscured beneath a hood, yet its presence radiated power.

Pyrrha instinctively tightened her grip on her sword, though she did not raise it. "Who are you?" she demanded.

"I am the Keeper of the Temple," the figure replied. "Guardian of the knowledge you seek."

Aleron straightened, bloodline is tied to this power, Pyrrha Infernal. The forces you face are not new— they have existed since the dawn of time. Your father's death was but another chapter in a war that has never truly ended."

She swallowed hard. "Then tell me how to end it."

The Keeper gestured toward the crystal on the altar. "The Heart of Aether holds the knowledge and the power you seek. But be warned—its wisdom does not come without cost."

Pyrrha hesitated. The weight of responsibility settled on her shoulders. She had come this far, faced trials that tested her very soul. Now, standing before the answer she had sought for so long, she wondered—was she truly ready for what came next?

Aleron placed a hand on her shoulder. His golden eyes met hers, steady and unwavering. "Whatever we face, we face together."

Pyrrha exhaled slowly, then reached for the crystal.

The moment her fingers brushed against it, the chamber was flooded with blinding light, and a voice—not the Keeper's, but something far greater—whispered into her very soul.

"Are you prepared to bear the burden of truth?"

 The voice echoed again, this time reverberating within Pyrrha's chest, shaking her very being. "Are you prepared to bear the burden of truth?"

She froze, the crystal pulsing in her hand as if alive, calling to something deep within her. Aleron stepped closer, his presence a steady anchor in the midst of the overwhelming force that surrounded them.

"Pyrrha," Aleron said softly, his voice filled with both caution and reassurance. "We came here together. Whatever this truth is, we will face it side by side."

Chapter Thirty-One: Power of the Crystal

Pyrrha's gaze flickered to him, and for a brief moment, she saw the same unwavering determination in his eyes that she had seen in her own reflection during the darkest of times. She felt his trust in her, and for a moment, the weight of the world seemed less heavy.

She took a steadying breath, her fingers tightening around the crystal. "I am ready," she said, her voice firm but laced with the uncertainty of the path ahead.

The light around them intensified, and the Keeper's voice once again resonated through the chamber. "Then, let the truth be revealed."

Suddenly, the crystal in Pyrrha's hand flared with a blinding white light, and visions—no longer mere flickers—unfolded before her eyes. She saw her father's death, but it was different from the memory she carried. It was not just the battle, not just the betrayal. No, there was something else—an ancient pact, a choice made long ago.

The vision shifted. Her father, the King, standing with a figure cloaked in shadow. The same dark sorcerer who had killed him. But this time, the vision lingered on something more—an exchange, an agreement forged in the name of balance, a sacrifice that was meant to preserve the kingdom. Pyrrha's heart clenched as she realised the truth: her father had not been a victim of an unforgivable betrayal. He had willingly sacrificed himself, knowing the consequences, knowing the cost.

The truth felt like a dagger to her chest, twisting in pain. "No," she whispered, shaking her head in disbelief. "He… he chose this?"

The Keeper's voice came again, this time less distant, almost mournful. "Your father knew the price of his decision, Pyrrha Infernal. The war between light and dark would never end, but he believed that his sacrifice would give his people a chance to live in peace, even if it meant his death."

Aleron's hand touched her arm, grounding her. "Pyrrha, this doesn't change the reason you fight. Your father's sacrifice is why you are here. His choice wasn't in vain."

But Pyrrha's heart felt torn. The path she had followed—the thirst for vengeance—had been built on a lie, on the belief that her father had been taken from her unfairly. What now? If he had known what would happen, if he had chosen this fate for himself, where did that leave her?

The light in the chamber dimmed, and the Keeper spoke once more. "To wield the Heart of Aether, you must accept the truth of your lineage, the truth of the burden that has always been yours. The choice that your father made was a piece of the puzzle, but now you must decide how you will move forward."

Pyrrha stood still, overwhelmed by the weight of it all. Her mission had been one of vengeance, but now the very foundation of her resolve had been shaken. She had been chasing a ghost, an illusion of justice.

And yet, there was still the war. Still the dark magic. Still the choices to be made.

She turned to Aleron, who watched her closely. "I don't know what to do with all of this," she admitted, her voice raw with emotion.

Aleron's expression softened, and he pulled her into a brief but comforting embrace. "Whatever you decide, you won't have to face it alone. We'll find our own way forward."

Pyrrha nodded, her mind racing, but for the first time, there was a flicker of hope amidst the confusion. She had the Heart of Aether now. The power to change everything was in her hands, but so too was the responsibility of what came next.

"Tell me more about the Heart," she said, stepping back, her voice stronger now. "What must I do to wield it properly?"

The Keeper raised its head, its glowing eyes studying her intently. "The Heart of Aether will grant you the power you seek, but beware. Its wisdom, its strength, can only be wielded by one who is prepared to face the darkest parts of themselves. Use it wisely or risk becoming the very thing you fight against."

Pyrrha's heartbeat like a war drum as the Keeper's words echoed in her mind. "Face the darkest parts of yourself." It felt like a warning, a challenge. She knew that the darkness she faced was not just the dark magic threatening her world, but the darker truths within herself—her rage, her thirst for vengeance, and the weight of a legacy that had always been beyond her grasp.

Aleron, sensing the conflict within her, gently placed a hand on her shoulder. "Whatever happens, Pyrrha, remember that you are not alone. This... this journey is as much about finding peace within yourself as it is about saving the world."

She turned to him, grateful for his support, but the gnawing uncertainty still lingered. She reached for the Heart of Aether once more, feeling its pulse against her fingertips, as if the crystal was aware of her inner turmoil.

"Keeper," Pyrrha asked, her voice steady despite the storm raging inside her, "what must I do to control its power?"

The Keeper stepped forward, its form shimmering in the dim light of the chamber. "To control the Heart of Aether, you must first accept your own truth. There is a balance that must be struck between the light and the dark within you. Only then can you unlock its full potential."

Pyrrha's mind raced. The light and the dark within her... What did that mean? Her desire for justice had pushed her this far, but had her pursuit of vengeance clouded her judgment? Had she become consumed by it, just as her father had warned her not to?

As if answering her unspoken question, the Keeper continued. "The Heart will test you, Pyrrha Infernal. It will show you visions of what could be, of what must be. But remember it does not choose for you. Only you can decide what path to follow."

Aleron's hand still rested on her shoulder, a silent promise of support. "You've faced unimaginable trials already, Pyrrha. You've made it this far. You've already proven that you can choose the right path."

Her breath caught as she thought of her father. His sacrifice. His unwavering belief in justice, even at the cost of everything he loved. Was she truly ready to follow in his footsteps? To embrace both the light and the dark within her?

With a final, resolute breath, Pyrrha turned her gaze back to the Heart of Aether. She knew what she had to do. The past could not be undone, but the future was still unwritten. She had the power to shape it, to use the Heart's strength to fight against the dark magic that threatened her world.

"Then I will choose," she declared, her voice steady and sure. "I will choose the path of justice. I will fight for my people, for my kingdom. And I will not let the darkness consume me."

The Keeper's form seemed to soften, a faint smile playing on its lips. "Then you are ready."

With those words, the chamber began to shimmer, the ancient symbols glowing brighter than ever. The Heart of Aether pulsed one final time, and Pyrrha felt a surge of power course through her, both invigorating and terrifying.

The vision of her father's sacrifice lingered in her mind, but now, it was accompanied by a sense of peace. She was no longer alone in this fight.

Aleron's voice brought her back to the present. "What now?"

Pyrrha turned to him, her eyes filled with a newfound resolve. "Now, we go back. There is still much to do."

The Keeper raised its hand one last time, and the golden doorway appeared, shimmering like a mirage. "The path ahead is not easy. But you, Pyrrha Infernal, have the strength to face whatever comes."

With that, Pyrrha stepped toward the doorway, Aleron by her side. As they crossed the threshold, the light from the temple faded, and they found themselves back on the mountain's edge, the cold wind biting at their skin.

Pyrrha looked out over the horizon, the weight of the world still heavy on her shoulders. But now, she had the power to shape its fate. The Heart of Aether was hers, and she would use it—wisely, carefully—to defeat the dark forces that sought to destroy everything she loved.

But one thing was certain: the battle was far from over. And this time, she would face it with the clarity of purpose her father had always hoped for.

Chapter Thirty-Two: The Path of Light and Shadows

The cold wind howled across the mountaintop, carrying with it the scent of distant storms. Pyrrha stood at the edge, the weight of the Heart of Aether heavy in her hand. Aleron stood beside her, his golden eyes scanning the horizon, as if searching for something that was not there. The world before them seemed impossibly vast, yet every inch of it felt fragile, like it could be shattered at any moment.

"We have the power," Pyrrha said, her voice barely above a whisper. "But it comes with a price. I can feel it, Aleron. The Heart is not just light. It's darkness too, woven into its very essence."

Aleron nodded, his expression solemn. "I understand. It is a burden. But it's the only way."

Pyrrha turned the crystal over in her hand, watching the glow shift and pulse. The Heart of Aether seemed to hum with an energy all its own, as if it were waiting for something. For her.

"We have to use it carefully," she continued, her voice tinged with resolve. "If we're not careful, we risk becoming the very thing we're fighting against."

Aleron reached out, touching her arm gently. "You're not alone in this. Whatever comes, we face it together."

Pyrrha's gaze softened as she met his eyes. The weight of his words settled within her, grounding her in the midst of the storm that raged in her heart. She was not alone. And she would not let the darkness consume her.

The journey back down the mountain was treacherous. The path was narrow and winding, and the further they descended, the more the air grew thick with unease. The world around them felt darker somehow, as though the shadows themselves were creeping in closer, waiting for the right moment to strike.

When they reached the base of the mountain, they were greeted by a strange sight—a small group of travellers gathered by the edge of the forest, their faces shrouded in mystery. Pyrrha's instincts flared, and her hand instinctively went to her sword, but Aleron held her back.

"Wait," he said softly. "Let's see who they are."

One of the travellers, a woman cloaked in tattered black robes, stepped forward. Her face was hidden beneath a hood, but her voice was unmistakably familiar—sharp, cold, and full of malice.

"Pyrrha Infernal," the woman said, her voice carrying a venomous edge. "I've been waiting for you."

A chill ran down Pyrrha's spine as she stepped forward, her eyes narrowing. "Who are you?"

The woman threw back her hood, revealing a pale, gaunt face with eyes that seemed to glow with an unnatural light.

"I am Morgath, a servant of the darkness you seek to destroy."

Aleron moved to stand beside Pyrrha, his hand resting on the hilt of his sword. "What do you want with us?"

Morgath smiled, a twisted, cruel smile that made Pyrrha's blood run cold. "I want nothing more than to see you fall, Pyrrha. To watch as your heart becomes as dark as the magic you fight against."

Pyrrha gripped the Heart of Aether tighter. The crystal's pulse seemed to quicken in her hand, as if sensing the danger that was closing in. She could feel the darkness swirling around her, but she knew she could not let it take control. Not now.

"We're not afraid of you," Pyrrha said, her voice unwavering. "And we will never fall to the darkness."

Morgath's smile faltered for a moment, but then her laughter echoed through the air, high-pitched and mocking. "You think you can stand against me, girl? You do not even know the true power of the Heart of Aether. It will consume you just like it consumes everything else. You can't fight fate."

With a flick of her wrist, Morgath summoned a burst of dark magic, sending it crashing toward Pyrrha and Aleron. The ground beneath their feet cracked and trembled as the magic collided with the earth, sending shockwaves of power through the air.

But Pyrrha was ready. She raised the Heart of Aether high, and a brilliant shield of light erupted around them, deflecting the dark magic with a force that sent ripples through the air. The Heart pulsed with energy, its light pushing back against Morgath's shadowy tendrils, but Pyrrha could feel the strain. The crystal was powerful, but it was also fragile, and its power was not infinite.

"We have to act fast," Pyrrha said, her voice tense. "If we don't, the Heart will drain us both."

Aleron nodded, drawing his sword. "I'll cover you. Do what

you must."

Pyrrha steeled herself, focusing on the Heart of Aether. She could feel the darkness within it, the same darkness Morgath wielded. But she would not let it control her. Not again.

"Take this!" Morgath hissed, her hands crackling with dark energy as she unleashed another wave of magic.

Pyrrha closed her eyes, drawing on the light and shadow within her. She could feel the crystal's power surging, but this time, it was different. She was not just using the Heart to shield herself. She was calling on its deepest power— the power to banish the darkness, to strike at the very core of Morgath's magic.

The Heart of Aether pulsed one final time, and a beam of radiant light shot forward, colliding with Morgath's magic in a brilliant explosion of light and shadow. The force of the

impact sent the dark sorceress sprawling backward, her form writhing in agony as the light consumed her.

For a moment, everything was still. The winds ceased, the earth settled, and the world seemed to hold its breath.

Then, Morgath's form dissolved into shadows, her scream echoing into the distance as her dark magic was erased from existence.

Pyrrha lowered the Heart of Aether, her chest rising and falling with each breath. She had won. But the battle was far from over. The dark magic was still out there, waiting for its next opportunity to strike.

Aleron stepped closer, his hand resting on her shoulder.

"We did it. But this is only the beginning, isn't it?"

Pyrrha looked out over the horizon, the weight of their mission pressing down on her once more. "Yes," she said softly. "It's just the beginning. But we will face it together, Aleron. We'll fight until the very end."
And as the sun dipped below the horizon, casting the world in twilight, Pyrrha knew that her journey was far from over. The darkness would not stop. But neither would she.

Chapter Thirty-Three: The Shifting Sands of Fate

The victory over Morgath had not been without its toll. Pyrrha could feel it in her bones, the lingering exhaustion from wielding the Heart of Aether's power. The light from the crystal had pushed back the shadows, but in doing so, it had left a faint but undeniable mark on her spirit. She couldn't shake the feeling that something else— something darker—had been awakened within her.

"Are you all right?" Aleron's voice broke through her thoughts, his gaze filled with concern.

Pyrrha nodded slowly, though her hand still gripped the Heart of Aether like a lifeline. "I'll be fine. It's just... the power is heavy. And Morgath's presence, even in defeat, lingers in the air. I can feel it."

Aleron stepped closer, his hand brushing against hers. The warmth of his touch steadied her. "We've won a battle, Pyrrha. But this war is far from over. The darkness will come again. And so will we."

She turned her gaze to the horizon, where the twilight sky bled into hues of purple and gold. "You are right. This is just a beginning. But I fear we're not prepared for what is next. The Heart of Aether... it's powerful, but I don't know how much longer it will hold."

"We'll find a way," Aleron said with quiet determination. "Together."

The sound of hoofbeats broke the silence, and both Pyrrha and Aleron spun around, alert. Emerging from the shadow of the trees was a lone rider—his silhouette unmistakable even in the dim light. Pyrrha's heart skipped a beat.

"Liora," she whispered under her breath.

The ethereal figure of Pyrrha's guardian appeared before them, her glowing wings folding behind her like radiant shields. Liora's expression was unreadable, her eyes filled with the weight of unspoken knowledge.

"My lady, my prince," Liora greeted them, her voice as calm as ever despite the tension in the air. "I bring news."

Pyrrha's heart quickened. "What news?"

Liora dismounted gracefully, her radiant wings retracting as she approached them. "The darkness you have faced is but a shadow of what is to come. There is a new threat— one that is more ancient and more insidious than Morgath. A force that seeks to twist the fabric of reality itself."

Aleron frowned. "What do you mean?"

Liora looked to Pyrrha, her gaze heavy with meaning. "The Heart of Aether is a beacon, Pyrrha. And it has attracted the attention of something far older than Morgath's kind— an entity that feeds on the power of the crystal. It seeks to bend the Heart to its will, and if it succeeds, it will bring about a new age of darkness."

Pyrrha's pulse quickened as the gravity of Liora's words sank in. "How do we stop it?"

Liora's expression was grim. "There is no simple answer. The only way to prevent the entity from claiming the Heart is to seek out the Oracle of the Lost Temple. But the Oracle is a being of riddles and illusions and finding it will not be easy. Even if you do, the Oracle may not give you the answers you seek."

Pyrrha clenched her fists. "Then we have no choice. We will find the Oracle."

Aleron stepped forward, his eyes narrowing with resolve. "We'll face whatever this new threat is. Together."

Liora nodded, her radiant wings shimmering in the fading light. "The road ahead is fraught with danger, but you must be prepared. Trust in your bond, Pyrrha. It will be tested more than ever before."

The tension in the air thickened, but Pyrrha felt a flicker of hope—a faint ember that burned brighter as the darkened path ahead grew clearer. The battle had only begun, and she would not stand idle. The Heart of Aether had brought her this far. But to protect it—and the world—it was time to seek answers beyond what they had known.

And so, they rode. Into the unknown. With the Heart of Aether guiding them, its light flickering like a lighthouse in a storm. Their journey would test them in ways they could not yet understand, but Pyrrha was resolute. No force— dark or light—would break her resolve.

Chapter Thirty-Four: The Oracle's Veil

The journey to the Lost Temple felt like a test in itself—one that stretched their resolve, patience, and trust. Each day seemed to bleed into the next, the landscape around them growing more desolate and mysterious, as though the very earth itself conspired to hide the secrets they sought. Yet through it all, the Heart of Aether remained a steady beacon, its soft glow the only constant in the ever-deepening shadows.

By the time they reached the foot of the mountain that concealed the Oracle's temple, the air was thick with anticipation. The peak loomed above them, shrouded in mist and cloud, as though even the heavens sought to veil what lay within. The ground beneath their feet grew rocky and treacherous, and the silence was broken only by the wind, whispering through the jagged peaks.

Pyrrha led the way, her sword at the ready, the Heart of Aether strapped to her side. Aleron rode closely behind her, his presence steady and unwavering. Despite the pressing urgency of their mission, there was an unspoken connection between them—an understanding that in the face of what was to come, they had no choice but to rely on each other.

"This place feels... alive," Aleron murmured, his eyes scanning the mountain around them. "As though it's watching us."

Pyrrha nodded, her own unease growing with each step. "I

feel it too. The Oracle is no ordinary being. We must be cautious."

They ascended in silence, the mountain's path growing steeper with every passing hour. As they neared the summit, a strange fog began to roll in, wrapping around them like a living thing. The air grew thick, as though the very atmosphere held its breath.

"Stay close," Pyrrha said softly. "This is it."

They crested the final rise, and before them stood a massive stone archway, half-swallowed by the fog. The entrance was adorned with carvings—runes and symbols of ancient power—glowing faintly in the twilight. The temple beyond was a shadowy silhouette, a structure carved directly into the mountain itself. It was as though it had always been there, waiting for them to find it.

Without a word, they dismounted and stepped forward, the weight of the moment pressing heavily on them both. As they passed through the archway, the temperature dropped sharply, and the fog thickened until they could barely see each other.

Then, a voice—soft, like a breeze—reached their ears. "Why have you come, children of fate?"

Pyrrha's heart skipped a beat, and she instinctively reached for her sword. "Show yourself," she demanded, her voice firm despite the chill that had settled in her bones.

The fog shifted, swirling like liquid around them, and from

within the mist, a figure appeared—a woman, or perhaps something more. Her form was translucent, shifting and flickering like the haze itself. Her eyes glowed with an inner light, ancient and unknowable, and her voice echoed from all directions.

"I am the Oracle," the figure intoned, "keeper of all that was, is, and will be. To seek my wisdom is to risk losing all that you hold dear. For knowledge, once revealed, cannot be undone."

Pyrrha stepped forward, her gaze unwavering. "We seek the truth. We must stop the darkness that threatens our world."

The Oracle's ethereal form regarded her for a long moment before she spoke again. "The Heart of Aether has brought you this far. But be warned, Pyrrha Infernal—its power is not meant to be wielded by any one soul. The burden it carries is too great for even you. And yet... you are bound to it, as is your fate."

Pyrrha's grip tightened around the Heart. "Tell me what I must do. I will bear whatever it takes."

The Oracle tilted her head, her eyes narrowing in scrutiny. "The path ahead is one of sacrifice. You must face the darkness within yourself and choose whether you will let it consume you or rise above it. Only by confronting your deepest fears can you hope to defeat the ancient force that seeks the Heart's power. But beware—the choices

you make will shape not only your future, but the future of all realms."

Aleron stepped forward, his voice steady despite the weight of the Oracle's words. "And if we fail?"

The Oracle's form flickered, and her eyes softened. "Then the world will fall into eternal night. The Heart of Aether will become the tool of darkness, and all that you love will be lost."

Silence hung heavy in the air. Pyrrha's heartbeat faster, the gravity of the Oracle's words pressing down on her like a physical weight. The fate of the world rested in her hands.

She closed her eyes for a moment, gathering her thoughts. When she opened them again, her gaze met Aleron's. His eyes held no fear—only determination.

"We will face whatever comes," he said softly. "Together."

Pyrrha nodded, her voice steady. "We will."

The Oracle's form shimmered, and for a moment, time itself held its breath. "Then go, children of fate. The time is near."

And with that, the fog parted, revealing the true depth of the temple—and the dark path that lay beyond.

Chapter Thirty-Five: The Heart's Reckoning

The Oracle's words haunted Pyrrha's thoughts as she and Aleron descended deeper into the heart of the temple. The mist had vanished, replaced by a heavy, suffocating stillness. The walls around them seemed to pulse with a strange energy, the very stones humming with ancient power. The path ahead was cloaked in shadows, yet the Heart of Aether glowed with a faint, unwavering light at her side.

They walked in silence, the weight of their journey pressing down on them both. Pyrrha's mind raced with the Oracle's cryptic warning—The Heart of Aether has brought you this far. But the burden it carries is too great for even you. Every step they took seemed to bring them closer to something inevitable, something they could not yet understand.

Aleron's hand brushed against hers, grounding her in the present. He gave her a quiet, reassuring smile. "Whatever happens, we face it together."

Pyrrha nodded, her grip on the Heart tightening. The crystal's energy thrummed beneath her fingers, almost as though it were alive. "I just... don't know what it means to carry such power."

"We'll find out," Aleron replied. "Together."

They reached the end of the stone corridor, where a massive door loomed before them. Carved with symbols and runes, it radiated an ominous energy. Pyrrha felt a chill run down her spine. This was the final trial.

She stepped forward, placing her hand on the door. The moment her fingers made contact, the door shuddered, then swung open with an agonizing slowness, revealing the chamber beyond.

Inside, the air was thick with shadow, and in the centre of the room stood an enormous, ancient altar, carved from black stone. Atop the altar lay the manifestation of their greatest fear—an immense, dark figure, its form shifting and flickering like smoke, its eyes glowing with malevolent light. The creature seemed to pulse with power, its very presence suffocating, as if it were feeding of their every emotion.

"You are the one who would dare challenge me?" the figure's voice boomed, a deep, mocking growl that reverberated through their bones.

Pyrrha's heart raced. "Who are you?" she demanded, her voice steady despite the fear threatening to overwhelm her.

"I am the force that lies beyond time, the darkness that has always existed, and the one who shall claim the Heart of Aether for my own," the figure hissed, its form flickering like a flame about to extinguish. "You have no idea what you face. The Heart will only destroy you. You cannot contain it. I will consume everything."

Aleron stepped forward, standing tall beside Pyrrha. "We will not let you win," he said, his voice firm, unwavering.

"The Heart is not yours to take."

The dark figure laughed, a sound that chilled them to their very core. "You cannot stop me. The Heart is already mine. It was always mine. And now, you will learn the price of your defiance."

The chamber began to tremble, the shadows swirling around them, growing thicker and more oppressive with every passing moment. The Heart of Aether flared with light, but it was weak, flickering like a dying star.

Pyrrha's breath quickened. She knew what had to be done, but she was not sure if she could bear the cost. The Oracle's warning echoed in her mind: You must face the darkness within yourself.

She closed her eyes, focusing on the warmth of Aleron's presence beside her, the strength of their bond. The darkness around them was a reflection of her own fears, her own doubts. If she gave in now, the darkness would consume them both.

Opening her eyes, she reached for the Heart. As her fingers touched the crystal, its light exploded with intensity, filling the chamber with blinding radiance. The darkness recoiled, screeching in pain as the light pushed back against it.

But even as the darkness writhed, Pyrrha could feel it pulling at her, trying to sink its claws into her soul. She

staggered, feeling herself slip toward the edge, but Aleron was there, his hand on her arm, steadying her.

"Don't let go," he whispered, his voice fierce with determination.

Pyrrha nodded, clinging to the Heart with every ounce of strength she had left. "I will not. Not now. Not ever."

With a cry of defiance, she focused all her energy into the Heart of Aether, pushing against the darkness. The crystal flared brighter, its power surging through her, flooding the chamber with light so pure it burned away the shadows.

For a moment, the world seemed to shudder, caught between light and darkness. Then, with a final, deafening roar, the dark figure collapsed into nothingness, its form disintegrating in the face of the overwhelming light.

The chamber fell silent.

Pyrrha collapsed to her knees, her breath ragged, every muscle in her body screaming from the exertion. The Heart of Aether was now dim, its power nearly spent.

Aleron knelt beside her, his hands gently pulling her into his arms. "You did it," he whispered, his voice full of awe and relief.

Pyrrha looked up at him, a faint smile playing at her lips. "We did it," she corrected softly, her gaze meeting his. "Together."

As the last remnants of the darkness faded away, the chamber began to quiet, the oppressive weightlifting from the air. The Heart of Aether, though dim, remained at her side—a silent reminder of the cost they had paid.

The future lay before them now… uncertain, but with a hope that had been rekindled by their courage and their bond.

Chapter Thirty-Six: The Final Choice

The world outside the temple seemed to hold its breath as Pyrrha and Aleron stepped into the light, the Heart of Aether cradled carefully between them. The darkness had been defeated, but the aftermath left them with a silence that stretched like an eternity. The power of the Heart was still within Pyrrha, but its glow had dimmed to a soft, pulsing rhythm—flickering like the last embers of a fire, barely alive.

Pyrrha's hands trembled as she held the crystal, and though the threat had passed, an unspoken weight still hung heavy in the air.

"What now?" she asked, her voice barely above a whisper. Her thoughts were clouded with uncertainty, the cost of their victory gnawing at her.

Aleron looked out into the horizon, where the distant peaks of the mountains seemed to reach for the heavens. The sun was beginning to set, painting the sky in hues of crimson and gold. The world felt at peace, yet Pyrrha knew that peace was fragile, fleeting. The Heart of Aether's power had been tested, but its true purpose was still unknown.

"Now we choose what to do with it," Aleron replied, his voice steady, but his gaze distant. "The Heart holds the power to change everything, Pyrrha. But it also carries a price. The power it gives... the temptation to wield it... it could consume us."

Pyrrha swallowed hard, the enormity of the decision pressing upon her chest. "What if we use it to restore balance? What if we use it to rid the world of the darkness for good?"

Aleron turned to her, his eyes filled with both love and concern. "And what if it consumes you instead? You have already felt its pull, Pyrrha. I have seen it in your eyes. It's a force that doesn't care who wields it. It takes what it wants, and it does not let go."

A heavy silence fell between them. Pyrrha's thoughts churned like a storm. The Heart had granted them both incredible power, and they had fought so hard to reach this moment. But now, standing on the precipice, the weight of their choices felt more daunting than ever.

The echoes of the dark figure's words still haunted her: The Heart will only destroy you. You cannot contain it. You will burn, as those before you have.

Yet, she had already defied the odds before. She had proven her strength, her resolve. But now, the future of the world lay in her hands, and she had to decide: could she control the Heart of Aether, or would it control her?

A soft breeze stirred the air, rustling the leaves of the trees around them. For a moment, it felt like time itself paused, holding its breath, waiting for her answer.

"You've already sacrificed so much," Aleron said quietly, his voice breaking through her thoughts. "If you choose to use the Heart, will it be worth it?"

Pyrrha looked into his eyes, her heart pounding in her chest. Her journey had been one of loss, pain, and sacrifice. She had fought for justice, for her father's memory, for the world she hoped to protect. But now, standing at the edge of everything, she wasn't sure if she could bear the cost of victory.

She closed her eyes, seeking the quiet space within her, where her father's voice still echoed in the distance, offering wisdom.

Justice demands sacrifices, Pyrrha. You may have to make choices that will haunt you. But remember, those who fight for what is right must stand firm—no matter the cost.

The weight of her father's words settled in her heart. She had come this far. She had lost so much already. But if she was to continue—if she was to honour his memory and her purpose—she had to choose with courage, not fear.

The Heart's light flickered, as if sensing her resolve. She looked at Aleron, and for a moment, the world seemed to fall away. They had faced every trial together. The darkness had tried to tear them apart, but it had not succeeded. Together, they could endure whatever came next.

"I won't let it consume me," Pyrrha said, her voice firm with newfound strength. "I will use it to restore balance. To end this war once and for all."

Aleron's eyes softened with admiration and concern. "If you do this, Pyrrha... we don't know what might happen."

"I've always known there were no guarantees," she replied, her gaze steady as she held the Heart before her. "But I will not stand by and let the darkness claim everything. The world deserves a chance."

With a deep breath, she raised the Heart of Aether to the heavens. The crystal pulsed with a renewed intensity, its light growing stronger and brighter, reaching into the very sky itself. The ground trembled beneath them as the power surged within Pyrrha, radiating outward in a brilliant burst.

For a moment, it felt as if the entire world was caught in the balance—light and shadow, hope, and despair, all woven together in a fragile thread.

Then, the light shattered, and the world fell silent.

Pyrrha collapsed to her knees, the Heart slipping from her grasp. Her body felt heavy, as though every ounce of energy had been drained from her. She could hear Aleron's voice calling her name, but it felt distant, muffled, as if she were underwater.

The darkness that had once threatened to consume her seemed to recede, but in its place, there was a new weight. A weight of choice—of sacrifice. Pyrrha had made her decision, and now, there was no turning back.

Aleron knelt beside her, his hand gently cupping her face. "Pyrrha, you've done it. The world is safe."

She blinked; her vision blurred. The world around them had changed, but the cost of that change was still sinking in. The Heart of Aether, its power spent, lay at her feet—a symbol of both victory and loss.

She had won. But at what cost?

The future was still uncertain, but Pyrrha knew one thing for certain now: she had given everything for this moment. And now, it was time to face whatever came next—together.

Chapter Thirty-Seven: The Dawn of New Beginnings

The silence that followed the burst of light seemed to stretch forever. Pyrrha's world had blurred, and her body felt as if it had been hollowed out. Every breath was a battle, and every heartbeat felt distant, as though the very rhythm of life had slipped away from her grasp.

But then, through the haze, she felt it—Aleron's hand, warm against her skin, his touch a lifeline pulling her back from the brink of darkness.

"Pyrrha," Aleron whispered urgently, his voice a beacon in the overwhelming stillness. "Pyrrha, look at me."

She forced her eyes open, struggling to focus as the world slowly came into view. The temple around them was still, bathed in the soft, dim light that now emanated from the Heart of Aether, which lay at her feet, no longer glowing with the same blinding intensity. It had spent its power— its purpose fulfilled, but the cost was heavy.

Pyrrha's breath caught in her chest, her body trembling as she tried to rise. Aleron helped her to her feet, his strength supporting her. The world was different now, but it was still the same. The balance had been restored, but Pyrrha could feel the weight of the choice she had made settling into her bones.

"The world… is it truly saved?" she asked softly, her voice weak but filled with a quiet resolve.

Aleron's gaze was steady, his golden eyes gleaming with a mixture of awe and uncertainty. "The darkness is gone. The Heart of Aether did what it was meant to. But…" He paused, as if weighing his next words carefully. "There is something about the balance that feels… different now. The power, the magic—it's not gone, Pyrrha. It is simply… changed."

Pyrrha nodded slowly, trying to process the magnitude of what had just happened. The world around her seemed more alive than ever, the air charged with an energy she had not felt before. But it was not the same as it had been when the Heart was at its full strength. The power had been absorbed into the world, scattered like seeds to be cultivated, to grow in new ways.

As she looked around, the symbols on the temple walls shifted and shimmered, a sign that the Heart's influence had extended beyond the chamber. The realm of light and shadow had been intertwined and now was reshaping itself. Pyrrha knew that the world they had fought for would never be the same, but it was a world that had been given another chance.

"Your father would be proud of you," Aleron said, his voice breaking through her thoughts. "You've done what no one thought was possible. You have given us a future."

Pyrrha turned her gaze toward him, her heart aching with the weight of his words. She had succeeded. She had avenged her father, restored balance, and stopped the darkness. But she had also lost so much along the way.

The weight of her journey, the sacrifices, the toll on her soul, all of it pressed against her chest, threatening to overwhelm her.

And yet, standing beside Aleron, feeling his unwavering support, something inside her stirred. There was still light ahead. She had been through the darkness, and now, there was a chance for something better.

"I've made so many choices," she whispered, "some that I will never be able to take back. But I did it for the world. For justice."

"You did it for us," Aleron replied, stepping closer. "And now... we face the future together. Whatever it holds."

For the first time, Pyrrha allowed herself a small, weary smile. The weight of the Heart, of the world, had lifted—at least for now. What remained was the uncertainty of the future. But for the first time in a long time, she did not feel alone in it.

Together.

They turned toward the temple's exit, and the world beyond, where the sun had risen higher, casting a golden glow over the land. The journey had been long and painful, but they had emerged victorious, not unscathed, but stronger for the battles they had fought.

And now, the world was theirs to rebuild, to shape, and to protect.

With one final glance at the Heart of Aether, which now

rested dormant on the altar, Pyrrha and Aleron stepped into the light, their path uncertain but their hearts steadfast.

As Pyrrha and Aleron stepped into the light, a flicker of unease tugged at the back of her mind, like the whisper of an old, forgotten danger. She glanced at Aleron, who met her gaze with a knowing look, his brow furrowing.

"There are things still out there, things we haven't yet understood," Pyrrha said quietly, almost to herself.

Aleron nodded, his voice soft but firm. "The balance we have restored is delicate. There are forces beyond what we have faced, and some will be watching, waiting."

Pyrrha's hand tightened around her sword, her resolve hardening. "Then we'll be ready."

But as they began their journey back toward the kingdom, the wind shifted—an omen of things to come. In the far distance, a dark shape loomed on the horizon, barely visible through the mists of dawn.

It was only a glimpse, fleeting—then it was gone.

But Pyrrha knew in her heart, the real fight was only just beginning.